FORBIDDEN

K. R. Burg

For my "first"
First Readers—
my students

PROLOGUE

The sunlight crept through the tall trees that stood silently in the forest. Except for the whisper of the wind, there was not a sound. Early spring buds clung to their branches, afraid to open completely and disrupt the serenity.

Suddenly there was a flicker of movement, darting around a tall oak, rustling the silent signs of late winter on the forest floor. The movement stopped for a brief moment.

"Alright, I give up," a tiny voice called out. "Where are you?"

Silence hung in the air.

"Lily, where are you?" the voice called out again, panic rising as the words dissipated into the thick stillness.

"Lily?" The word was barely a whisper as the young boy held his breath.

"Here!" A mushroom moved, and a fairy stepped forward. "Could not find me, could you?"

"That was not nice of you." The young boy flew down and stood next to her, his hands on his hips, sulking. "Plus, here I do not like to be."

"In the forest?" Lily turned and jumped up to the top of the mushroom, sitting down. "All the words Father says—to scare us, it is. I have never had any trouble…" Lily realized her mistake as soon as the words were spoken.

"Before now you have been here?" Del looked at her.

"Well, yes I have," Lily stuck out her chin, defiantly. "And no troubles I have had. None."

Del flew up to a branch and playfully inched his way along the piece of wood, as though he were performing a high-wire act. "Father speaks the truth, I should think. He has your well-being in mind." He sat down and stared at his sister, waiting for her response.

Lily walked out a ways from the trunk of the tall oak, and stood looking up at her younger brother. He was so handsome. All of the young maiden fairies giggled with delight whenever he entered a room. Yet, he was also so practical—something that she herself was not, nor ever could be.

"To protect us is Father's concern…" she began, looking down at her feet.

"No, to protect you, future queen," Del interrupted her. Instantly, Lily's ears began to burn with embarrassment. Del was right. She was the one chosen to be the future queen of the fairies. She had lived this reality every day, constantly reminded that her life was already planned for her.

"I know, I know," Lily mumbled, kicking at the patches of moss in front of her. "Unfair it is when I have no choice. Can you not understand how I feel?" She looked up at Del, sitting on the branch, wanting his approval. Instead, she saw a look of dread, of fear on his face. His eyes were wide, his mouth open.

"Lily, look out!" Del cried out, but it was too late. A gigantic net crashed down upon Lily, smothering her with its weight. She struggled to fly away, but her wings only became tangled in the mesh.

"What do we have here?" A strange voice boomed out above her. Lily tried to right herself, but the mesh kept pushing her down.

"What is it?" another voice squeaked out loudly. "A dragonfly?"

"If it is, it's the weirdest dragonfly I've ever seen," the booming voice returned, hurting Lily's ears. She righted herself, only to tumble into the open air, landing on the surface of a plump hand, which quickly closed around her, causing her to gasp for breath.

"What should we do with it?" the squeaky voice asked as he bent down to look at the foreign object enclosed in the hand.

"I say we leave it," the booming voice replied as he opened his hand just a bit. Lily caught her breath again and opened her eyes, but then was thrown back by a sudden, searing burn as a large hand ripped away her left wing. She doubled over in pain, unable to make even a sound. The hand opened up, and she toppled over the edge, falling to the ground with a thud. She lay in the foliage, not moving.

"It isn't going anywhere anyhow." The booming voice laughed as it walked away, leaving Lily to the quietness of the forest. She heard Del's voice frantically calling out to her, but she was unable to open her eyes or respond. Just as she was about to drift into unconsciousness, she felt herself gently lifted up and wrapped in warmth. She opened her eyes, only to look into two large, blue pools that spoke only of kindness.

"Help me," she whispered, and then her eyes closed.

CHAPTER ONE

60 years later

Emma Campbell was upset. Very upset.

It wasn't because she was sitting in the passenger seat of her mother's SUV, moving with the gentle country hills as though she were on a kiddy roller coaster ride. It had nothing to do with the fact that her mother insisted on singing to a lame country song crooning from the radio that told of the woes of every broken heart. And the incessant growling now coming from her empty stomach was not the reason for her sour mood.

It had everything to do with the fact that the destination of their short journey was the large house belonging to Emma's grandmother—her quirky, strange, unusual grandmother. Emma sighed as she remembered how, on many different occasions, Grams embarrassed her.

The most recent event had been her birthday party. Emma had been so excited at the thought of having her friends over for a party, complete with pre-teen activities that all girls would enjoy. She had helped in the planning, of course, and her m had bent the rules "just this once" to include things that Emma wanted. After all, Emma argued, a girl doesn't turn thirteen every year.

Everything was going great—until Grams showed up. She galloped right into the backyard and presented Emma with her gift. A dress-up doll. Something that a five-year-old would be excited about, not a teenager. Emma's face turned red as the other girls snickered quietly. Even though she cringed inside, she knew what her parents expected her to do. She turned to Grams and forced a smile on her face.

"Thanks, Grams," Emma said in a monotone voice. "It's great." Grams clapped her hands with excitement.

"Oh, I hoped that you would like it!" she cried. "All the young girls have one now."

Yeah, *young* girls, Emma thought. Not teenagers.

"Come on, Em," Trudy Campbell's voice brought Emma back to reality. She glanced at her daughter as they made their way down the country road. "You know that I have to go to this work conference, and it's just for the weekend. Two nights, that's all. It'll be okay. Besides, Grams is excited to see you."

Yeah, Emma thought, Grams is *always* excited to see me.

Trudy announced their arrival by steering the SUV into a long driveway bordered by arborvitae, the towering coniferous trees leading the way up to the white plantation-style house. As they crept up the long drive, Emma looked over the estate she had visited many times. The house itself was surrounded by a large, colorful garden that could have come right from a Monet Impressionist masterpiece. Even though it was still spring, various colors were already in bloom. Behind the garden stood a lush forest that spread for what seemed like miles. The trees, although green with the season, appeared to change to darker hues the farther back her eyes traveled.

The SUV stopped in front of the house. As Emma climbed out of the car, she was greeted with a sudden commotion coming from the garden.

"Here you are!" cried an elderly woman as she dropped her garden tools, and galloped across the lawn toward the visitors. Emma took a quick look at her grandmother. Lila Campbell's outfit consisted of a flowery dress and apron, large work boots, dirty garden gloves, and a floppy sun hat that did little to hide the long silver braid hanging down her back. Emma gave her mother a quick glance, complete with rolling eyes. Trudy Campbell returned the glance with one of her own, silently communicating a "be nice" message to her daughter. Emma sighed once again.

"Lila, it's so good to see you," Trudy said as she went to hug her mother-in-law. Lila Campbell returned the embrace, and then turned to Emma.

"There is my big girl!" she said as she pulled Emma into a strong hug. Emma silently winced at her grandmother's greeting.

"Hi, Grams," she said, stepping back and sliding her hands into her jeans.

"A wonderful day for visitors, it is indeed!" Lila said as she ushered them into the house, her hands waving in the air as though she were directing a symphony. Emma lagged behind as the two women chatted with each other. Emma stood in the entranceway and slowly looked around the kitchen. There were small planters of ivy, African violets, primrose, and various herbs everywhere in the room—on the window ledges, the table, and the counters. It was as though the room itself was a garden, full of color, fragrance, and life. Only when her eyes reached the covered table did she understand the expectations of the visit—small chat, tea, and week-old cookies—all things that she could do without. Scout, the household cal-ico, rubbed her body against Emma's leg, crying for attention.

"Oh, dear," Lila said, noticing Emma's expres-sion. "Tea is not your thing, I suppose."

Emma shrugged, bending down to give the cat a quick scratch behind the ears. Scout responded with a deep-throated purr.

"Bring your things upstairs, then, and choose your room," Lila said. "Any of the guest rooms is open."

Emma nodded, picked up her backpack and trudged up the flight of stairs to the second floor. In all of her years visiting her grandmoth-er's house, Emma had never stayed in any of the upstairs bedrooms. Usually the visits were for a few hours, never overnight, and much of the time had been spent downstairs or outside. The upstairs was new territory for her. She glanced in the first room on the left, only to be greeted with a pink-lace canopy bed, stuffed animals, and a very large dollhouse.

Definitely not for me, Emma sighed. She contin-ued down the hallway to the adjoining bedroom. It was more toned down than the first, and offered a full-size bed, a rocking chair, and an antique rolltop desk in the corner. It was simple and quaint, and was almost a sure thing—until Emma sat on the bed and discovered the constant squeaking the springs made. The room quickly became a distant memory as she moved to the next bedroom.

This room was much smaller than the first two. In fact, Emma had a hard time believing that it was indeed a bedroom. It had the feeling of a cozy study area or a small library. The walls were covered with a striped sage print that brought out the natural dark woodwork framing the room. Next to the large window overlooking the colorful garden and forest was a daybed covered with a plain duvet. In the corner was an antique chaise lounge and reading lamp. Emma set her backpack on the daybed and sat down, thankful that there were no squeaks to welcome her. She noticed a door on the right side of the room and opened it. Inside was a small closet area, empty of any belongings. Straight ahead was another full-size door. Emma opened it and peered inside. Even in the absence of direct light she could see that the door led to another level, probably an attic. She slowly began to climb the steep, wooden staircase, making sure to leave the door open.

Emma reached the top of the stairs and stopped. This room was much larger than she had imagined, going from one end of the house to the other. The old, wooden floor creaked as she cautiously walked over to some boxes. Dust covered just about every-thing in the room.

This is not going to be good for my allergies, she thought.

She walked carefully down a narrow aisle, look-ing at the items displayed. Old military outfits hung from the rafters. A faded quilt, carefully folded, partially covered a stack of worn books. A bent Christmas tree, the ornaments still hanging from it, leaned against a wall in the corner. A large an-tique mirror was propped up against an old dresser. Emma stopped in front of it. She could hardly see into the mirror, it had so much dust covering it. Her hand slowly sliced through the thick layer resting on the surface, sending pewter gray particles into the air. She instantly closed her eyes, and waited for the dust to settle.

Using the one clear spot on the mirror, Emma examined herself. Her light brown, wavy hair wasn't anything to cheer about, especially when it was hu-mid outside. While she would constantly try to tame it, the mousy strands had a mind of their own, usu-ally ending up in some sort of frustrated ponytail. Her freckles didn't help either—definitely a gift from her mother. With time, the freckles on Trudy Campbell's face had faded, leaving behind a picture of sophistication and class. Emma secretly longed for that day, concluding as she stared into the mirror with her bluish-green eyes that she was just plain.

Emma's eyes then fell on a rocking horse, complete with saddle and cowboy hat, that was behind her. Tears instantly welled up as she realized the rocking horse was probably once used by a boy—James P. Campbell, in fact.

"Dad." Emma choked up as the words escaped her lips. It had only been six months since the accident, but she found herself still crying at the thought of him–the thought of him never coming home again. He had been her rock, her fortress. It was he who taught her to ride a bike and throw a baseball. It was he who teased her about boys, and told her that he believed in her. It was he who tucked her into bed each night, every night—even the night before the…a tear slid down Emma's cheek. He was never coming home again.

Her eyes wandered to an open box next to the rocking horse. Emma bent down and picked up the top object. It was a used comic book with a superhero on the front cover. She leafed through a few pages, put it aside, and picked up the next comic book.

I never knew Dad was into comic books, she thought to herself as she studied the book. Although she preferred fiction, she had to admit that the comic books were pretty entertaining.

Time went by, and Emma eventually sat down, finding a comfortable position against an old recliner. The storyline of the superhero comic books had drawn her in, and she didn't want to leave the attic.

Maybe if I take a few with me, I will have something to read later tonight, she concluded. As she was digging through the box, gathering a few books for herself, she came across a leather-bound journal. She held it in her hands, examining it.

"What is this doing here?" she asked herself. She opened the book, yellowed pages greeting her. She instantly recognized the handwriting. It was her father's writing, a bit younger looking, but showing the same confidence he always had in everything he had accomplished. She turned to the first page.

> *Dear Journal,*
> *So, I am supposed to start a story and add to it a little each night. "Something original," my teacher says. Right. Nothing original has ever happened to me. That's the problem…nothing original.*

Emma smiled. She envisioned a much younger version of James P. Campbell lying on his bed one night, scribbling these words into the new journal. She tucked the leather-bound book into the pile of comic books and moved to stand up. As she stepped toward the stairs, though, her foot caught a loose floorboard. Emma stumbled backwards and fell onto the floor, knocking objects over in her path, and slightly bruising her knee in the process. She silently chided herself as she rubbed her knee, knowing that her pride hurt much more than the tender skin she focused on.

Emma slowly began to pick up the objects around her that had fallen over, and gather the books she intended to take with her. Suddenly she caught sight of a small, wooden box on the floor next to her. She held it up, turning it around. The box appeared to have been carved from one piece of wood, the sides displaying intricate detail. Emma carefully lifted the lid of the box, only to discover a collection of items inside.

"What is this?" Emma said out loud as she picked up one item. It was a golden ring that sparkled, even in the dull attic light. It was beautifully carved; gold ringlets that intertwined throughout the ring blazed in the light. Even the ringlets appeared to have minute carvings on them, displaying a superior level of artistry. Emma slid the ring onto her pinky finger and gasped. The ring fit perfectly.

She turned her attention to another mystery item—a small insect wing. It was no more than the length of her thumb, and translucent in nature. As she examined it closely, she realized that the wing shimmered depending on the angle at which it was held.

Just then Emma's thoughts were interrupted by her mother's voice calling her. She quickly returned the items to the box, and descended the stairs, leaving the comic books and journal on her bed for further discovery. Upon entering the kitchen once again, she found the two women where she had left them, chatting over the same tea and cookies.

"Did you choose your room?" Lila said as she rose to pour more tea for herself and Trudy. Emma revealed her choice to the two women.

"Oh, the room for reading! That room…oh, I do love that room," Lila said as she pushed the cookie tray towards Emma.

"Grams, I found the door to the attic in the closet," Emma said.

"Yes, many older homes had attic doors leading off of bedrooms and closets," Lila said as she poured more tea for herself. "A hassle it has been, though—trying to haul everything up those steep stairs."

"Well, it seems like you hauled a lot up," Emma said in an honest tone, causing both women to laugh. "There is a lot of stuff up there, Grams, but I guess I am interested most, though, in knowing the story behind the wooden box."

"The box? Which box?" Lila handed Trudy her cup and saucer. "Many boxes are up there."

"You know," Emma said, "the small wooden box that has a ring inside."

For a moment, not a sound could be heard in the kitchen. Lila's puzzled face looked at Emma, and then realization set in. Her cup and saucer fell from her hands and crashed onto the hard floor, and she instantly covered her mouth. Trudy looked at Emma, perplexed by what was occurring.

"The ring?" Lila said.

Emma was confused. "Grams, you know—the wooden box that has the ring..." She was interrupted by Lila's gasp as she walked over and stood in front of her granddaughter.

"Emma, you must tell me the truth," Lila whispered in a low, anxious voice that only Emma could hear. Her now pale face was inches away from Emma's own, peering into Emma's. "Did you touch it? Did you touch...the ring?"

CHAPTER TWO

For as long as she could remember, Emma had not been good at one important survival skill—lying. No matter how hard she had tried, she had never mastered the craft.

"Em, you're biting your lip again," her father would remind her when she was faced with the choice of telling the truth or spinning a web of deception. It was a telltale sign—that and the fact that her face would sometimes look flushed while she contemplated her options. Secretly, her parents were thankful that she did not excel at this vice.

It was this thought that filled Emma's mind as her grandmother now stood in front of her.

"Emma, did you touch the ring?" Lila Campbell asked again, this time a bit louder. Emma's face instantly felt warm, and her teeth began to nibble on her bottom lip. Her eyes rose to meet her grandmother's, and she slowly nodded.

"I just put it on my pinky finger," she said. Her thoughts were conflicted. She knew that she shouldn't have taken the box that was currently tucked in her front sweatshirt pocket, but she wanted to have more time to look at the objects. I'm just borrowing it for now, she told herself.

Lila Campbell took a step back, and exhaled slowly. She took Emma's hands in her own and managed to smile at the confused girl standing in front of her.

"It's alright, dear. What's done is done," she said quietly, more to herself than her confused guests. Suddenly, her attitude changed.

"No harm done that a cookie can't undo!" Lila said, smiling as she pushed the tray of cookies toward Emma and then joined Trudy at the table. Soon chatter once again filled the room.

Emma stood off to the side, carefully taking in what had just happened. She slid her hand into her front sweatshirt pocket, relieved when her fingers touched the hardness of the box. Why did Grams get so upset? What was the story behind the ring? And why was there an insect wing in the mysterious box? Unfortunately, her mind filled with more questions than answers.

Emma's thoughts were interrupted by the movement of the two women as they got up from the table.

"I should be back by dinner Sunday night," Trudy reminded Lila as they walked to the front door. "If you need to contact me, you have my number." Trudy's arms surrounded Emma in a farewell embrace as she whispered in Emma's ear, "I hope you have a good time."

Emma nodded and shrugged as her mother climbed into the driver's seat. As the SUV drifted out of sight, Emma stood in the middle of the driveway, wondering just how she had arrived alone at the one place she did not want to be—her grandmother's house.

Emma turned on the reading light next to her bed. It was late, but she couldn't sleep. Perhaps it was Gram's reaction to her question that was bothering her. It wasn't a normal reaction. Why had Grams become so upset about something so trivial?

Because that is Grams, Emma concluded to herself as she took the wooden box from its hiding place in her backpack. She opened the lid and examined the two objects again, not touching them. They were unusual objects to have in a house, she thought.

Why would Grams hold onto them, and why would she place them in the attic?

Too many questions churning in her head made it impossible for Emma to consider sleep. She returned the box to its hiding place and pulled out a book to read. The comic books, as entertaining as they were, were not calling her. Instead, she held the leather journal in her hands. The leather was indeed worn, held together by a metal clasp that was also worn with age. It smelled of dust and dirt and sweat, all the things that reminded her of her father. Just seeing his handwriting made him feel close by. Tears formed in her eyes, but she quickly wiped them away. She wanted to see what was written.

Nothing original at all. I do have this dream off and on. People say that your dreams tell something about you. I don't know if that's true, but it's a start on writing this assignment. There is a boy—he's young. Maybe about six or seven years old, I think, and he is playing baseball in the backyard. He throws the ball up and then catches it, and then throws it up again, but it goes over the fence into the forest. The fence that his mom says to never go through...insert creepy music here. (Are you kidding me? I've only been writing for 10 minutes???! This assignment is going to kill me.) The boy does what any boy would do—he goes into the forest to get his baseball. But then there is a swarm of butterflies surrounding him, and he follows them. They were all different colors, and I guess, if you were a girl, you would even say they were "pretty" although you didn't hear me using that word, ok?

Anyway, the butterflies lead the boy far into the forest. He comes to this open clearing and he stands there. Just then, there is glowing light, and then a bright flash and

(30 minutes. I am done.)

What a strange story, Emma thought to herself. Scout jumped up on the bed and curled up under the journal. Emma absentmindedly stroked her head, and then turned the page. She read late into the night, and when she was done, she closed her eyes, the open journal still in her hand.

CHAPTER THREE

"This bluish purple one right here? It is called delphinium—my favorite flower of all," Lila said as she pointed to a tall, colorful spike of small flowers towering above the rest of the garden. Emma simply nodded and continued to work the soil around the edge of the shorter plants. The spring sun stood high above, and small beads of sweat were forming on her brow. She wiped her forehead with the back of her borrowed garden glove, unknowingly leaving a trail of dirt behind. She had been working out in the garden for more than an hour, mainly because there wasn't much else to do. Every couple of minutes Lila would chirp about various plants in the garden; Emma just listened.

"This one here," Lila said, pointing out a large, multilayered pale pink flower, "is a peony. Isn't it beautiful?" She bent down and sniffed the flower, sighing with contentment. Emma shrugged, looking at her grandmother. She wondered how someone could enjoy being around bugs and dirt so much. She looked out at the thick forest, so close to the garden. For all of the years that she had been visiting, Emma couldn't remember one time that she had actually gone into the forest.

"It is a pretty forest, isn't it?" Lila's words interrupted her thoughts. "I do love living so close to the woods. It's….comforting."

"Grams, do you ever take walks in the forest?" Emma said.

The clippers in Lila's hands fell silent as she looked off into the woods. "Walks in there I don't take anymore," she finally said quietly. Emma was surprised and looked at her grandmother, who was still gazing into the woods. It wasn't the words that Lila had used, but rather the tone—Emma recognized the tone because her mother had used the same expression often since her dad had died. Sadness. Emma knew that she should probably drop the matter, but she couldn't give up that quickly.

"But why not, Grams?" Emma didn't dare look at her grandmother, knowing full well that her face would give her away, but instead focused her attention on the same patch of dirt she had been attending to for the last ten minutes or so.

"Oh," Lila shook her head as she snapped out of her seriousness. "You know—too many mosquitoes." Emma was puzzled. Mosquitoes? That didn't seem like such a big problem, Emma thought to herself. Hadn't Grams ever been camping? After all, that's what bug spray was for.

"Gardening is not your thing either, is it?" Lila said, leaning on a shovel.

"Not really," Emma said. "Plus, it is a bit hot out here, Grams."

"My dear, you are right!" Lila said, cheerfully, showing her old self once again. "Go inside and wash up a bit, and have a glass of the lemonade I just made. I will be in shortly."

Emma didn't wait to see if the conversation would continue. She was already walking on the lush, green grass when she glanced back at her grandmother, still working on pruning the taller plants and deadheading the flower-bearing ones. She had to admit it—Grams did have a way with flowers. The garden was filled with different colors in bloom. There were also bright birdhouses placed throughout the large area, attracting various kinds of flyers. Wind chimes, hanging from tall, wooden poles located in the middle of the garden, sent soft notes of welcome floating through the air.

As she walked around the back of the house, her hand instinctively went to her jean pocket, pulling out the golden ring that had been hidden deep within. Emma paused and looked at the ring. Gram's strange response still warranted an answer; Emma wanted more time to examine the ring. She tucked the ring back in her pocket and opened the patio door, only to be greeted with a sudden flash of white, orange, and gray.

"Scout—no!" Emma exclaimed, but the cat was too quick, scooting past her legs and running down the patio toward the forest. The cat stopped at the edge, turned back, and looked at Emma, checking to see if she would follow. Then it jumped silently off the patio and ran into the woods.

Emma looked at the cat, and then toward the garden. She could just make out Lila's garden hat slowly moving among the taller plants, her distant singing letting Emma know that she planned to work among the flowers for a bit longer. Emma sighed. She had already managed to displease her hostess once by mentioning the ring. She did not want to be blamed for letting her grandmother's house cat out, even if it was an accident. Mosquitoes or no mosquitoes, she had no choice but to chase after the fugitive feline.

"Scout!" Emma called out as she disappeared among the tall trees. She continued jogging along the narrow pathway, looking both left and right for any sight of the cat, but to no avail. Although it was much cooler in the forest, the absence of bright light did not help in the search.

Emma soon came to a small clearing in the woods. The sun gently caressed the forest floor, causing the thick carpet of trillium to stand silently at attention. She wandered to the middle of the clearing and stood still, looking all around her. The trees were silent, their branches not daring to move. Not a sound could be heard. The clearing was still—too still. Beyond the trees the sunlight was blocked out as darkness veiled the unknown. Emma turned to see the path where she had come, but it wasn't there. An uneasy feeling began to grow deep inside her. Something wasn't right. She turned and glanced in all directions.

It had just been here, she thought frantically, but it was no use. The path had simply vanished. It was then that Emma realized she wasn't alone.

Without any notice, a dark, foul mist began to form around the outer edges of the clearing. Slowly it encircled the circumference of the clearing. There was no way out. The mist grew darker, slowly swallowing up the dim sunlight. Emma gasped, and took a step back. She watched it as it slithered around the trees, creeping up the branches as though it were a single, living entity, its movements reminding her of serpents hunting their prey. A chill ran through Emma; the closer the mist came, the colder she was. She wanted to scream and run, but she couldn't. Her voice and legs were frozen. She didn't move. She didn't breathe. She tried not to blink. She only watched as it came closer and closer, her eyes wide with fright. The beating of her heart and gasps for breath competed with the hissing sounds of the smoke surrounding her.

When the acrid smoke reached her, it morphed into various shadows and surrounded her. The shadows moved independently of one another, taunting her, scaring her, whispering evil all around her. The shadow directly in front of her now had what appeared to be an abstract face and two arms. The blurry face suddenly grew horrendously large, stretching high above her. It snarled and bared large, sharp fangs. Only inches from Emma's face, the shadow formed tentacles that curled around her nose and neck. Emma felt herself being pulled toward the creature. She tried to fight it, but it was slowly squeezing the air from inside her. Just when she thought she was going to pass out, the trillium on the forest floor began to dance, swaying back and forth, shooting light sprays into the air.

The light quickly gathered around Emma, separating her from the darkness. The sprays wove themselves into a warm, protective capsule, lifting her off the forest floor and carrying her at break-neck speed through the mist and deep into the forest. Emma looked back, only to see the dark creatures chasing her, their rumbling anger sending out cries that sounded like metal on metal.

Emma lifted her head and watched as the light sprays changed their direction. It was then that Emma saw a large boulder off in the distance. It glowed, pulsing like a lighthouse on a stormy night. The capsule changed course again and headed directly for the boulder.

We aren't slowing down, Emma realized, snapping to attention. *I'm going too fast...we're going to...NO!*

But she didn't finish her thoughts, for she was interrupted by her own screams as the glowing stone engulfed her.

CHAPTER FOUR

Lila Campbell had always been fond of flowers. From the time that she was young, she couldn't remember a day without them. She felt alive when she was in her garden, nurturing the young plants and encouraging the struggling ones, just as she was doing now.

She smiled as she remembered how Garrett had watched her each day in the garden. They could spend time together outside, not talking—just being together. That was the way they were—living out a quiet, loving companionship over a period of fifty-four years. Many times she would work, only to look up and see Garrett smiling at her. Oh, and he had such a great smile! His smile would permeate deep into his blue eyes. Lila sighed. She missed that smile.

It had been almost seven years since Garrett had become ill. He never complained once while he was sick, but she had fought the illness, fought it hard by creating new remedies and organic meals and always being by his side. She wasn't fond of doctors and tended to rely on her own knowledge of plants. That had always worked for her before.

Secretly, she had always thought that she would be the first one to die, because of her condition. But now Garrett was gone, and she was alone, alone with her flowers and the big, sprawling, empty house. There had been times that James and Trudy had tried to convince her to sell, but she had politely resisted.

"Mother, it's too big for you," James said, "and the upkeep is unreasonable."

"Move closer to us," Trudy said. "We would love to see you more often."

Although they meant well, she knew that they just didn't understand. After all, this was the only home that she had ever known. Garrett grew up in this house, and it was hers as well. She couldn't leave it now. It was all that she had left of him.

Now, as the afternoon sun beat down on Lila, she was suddenly startled by a gust of chilling wind that came out of nowhere. She glanced up and instantly realized that, while she had been daydreaming, it had become quite dark within the woods. In fact, the trees seemed to disappear as the darkness blended together, but stopped at the edge where the forest ended and the garden began.

Something isn't right, she thought to herself as the garden tools fell to the ground. Her legs moved quickly as she advanced toward the house. Her heart beat rapidly as she approached the back door, only to stop suddenly. There, in front of the door stood Scout, meowing incessantly. The frightened cat confirmed her fears. Something was wrong.

"Emma?" Lila said as she entered the house, searching for her granddaughter. She quickly scanned the rooms, both upstairs and down, and realized that, without the presence of muddy footprints and an empty lemonade glass, Emma had not entered the house. Where was she?

Lila quickly ran out the back door and stopped on the porch steps, looking all around. Her eyes fell on the darkened forest in front of her.

The forest.

Emma had gone into the forest.

"No…." the word escaped Lila's lips like air slowly leaving an inflated balloon. Before her mind could think, she ran toward the forest, only to stop suddenly at the edge. What would happen when she crossed over? Would the darkness be waiting for her, too?

Lila knew that she couldn't think about these questions. Emma was in trouble. Her granddaughter needed her. She placed one foot on the forest floor, only to be thrown back by a force so powerful, it knocked her to the ground. Lila lay on the ground, gasping for breath.

"Help her," she whispered, and then her eyes closed.

⇥⊹ ⊹⇤

The boy wakes up in a meadow. It's still day, but there are fireflies flying around. (I know that's a little strange—fireflies in daytime, but I am just writing the story down.)

Yes, it's taken me 30 minutes to write this much down. Watching TV while you're supposed to be doing homework sometimes does that to you. (Besides, I have a hard time believing that my teacher will even read this anyways.)

--JPC

CHAPTER FIVE

The first realization Emma had that something significant had happened was the tingling numbness that swept throughout her whole body. She lay still, focusing only on the act of breathing. It should have been a natural thing, something the body automatically does, and yet it took every ounce of Emma's concentration. The numbness slowly gave way to a dull ache that exhausted every living cell of her being. Nothing compared to this aching—not even the time that Emma had been thrown from a horse while at camp and had spent three days in bed recuperating.

She continued to lay still, taking in the sounds around her. They were familiar, and yet different. She recognized the sound of wind chimes, but it was almost as though they were whispering, not wanting to be heard. Emma's foggy brain caught disconnected words mingling with the sounds.

"Is she alive?"

"…don't know…"

"…must help her…"

"…use this…carefully now…not too much…"

Emma felt her bottom lip being pulled back, and a sweet, fruity liquid gently poured along her gum line. Slowly the dull ache began to evaporate from her veins, and strength took its place. Her bottom lip snapped back into place, and for the first time, Emma breathed in deeply.

When she mustered enough strength to open her eyes, she saw only blue sky above. Her eyes were having trouble focusing, and her peripheral vision was filled with blurred images moving quickly about. She was aware that she was not alone, but still too exhausted to cry out. Tinkling sounds continued to fill the air, reminding her of Gram's garden.

That's it, she thought to herself. I must have fainted from the heat, and Grams is trying to help me.

"Hello! In there are you?" Emma suddenly felt a tiny pecking on her forehead. Her eyes flew wide open, only to be blocked by an object flying in her vision path. She instantly sat up (much too quickly, she realized), hitting the object with her forehead, sending it high into the air. Wind chimes echoed all around her. Emma's head hurt badly and groaning, she slowly closed her eyes again.

"Well, alive you are—at least," a tiny voice said above her. Emma slowly opened her eyes again and concentrated on focusing. A creature was hovering above her. Emma cried out and instantly skirted away.

"Who…what…are…you?" she gasped. The creature followed her, and she frantically crawled away again, her body screaming in pain with each move. The creature did not follow her this time, but stayed a distance away. Emma sat on the ground, breathing heavily, keeping her eyes trained on the fluttering creature.

After some time, Emma's heart rate and vision returned to normal, and she was able to think clearly. She deducted that the creature was, in fact, a girl. She was dressed in a flowing gown, the hue of which was a deep gold. Her eyes were the color of burning embers. Her ivory complexion was a stark contrast to the raven black hair that softly swayed back and forth with her movements. It wasn't, however, the physical, humanly appearance that Emma instantly noticed. Instead, it was the girl's wings, which beat so rapidly, it almost appeared that they weren't moving at all. Even though her head still hurt, Emma was alert enough to realize that the wings, translucent in nature, shimmered in the sunlight.

"Important questions you must answer," the fairy girl said as she moved only inches away from Emma's face. "The first is why in the forest you were."

Emma stammered, trying to remember. "I…I was looking for my grandmother's cat."

"Cat?" a young girl fairy asked. "What is a cat?"

"You are a cat?" asked a young boy fairy who suddenly flew upon the scene.

"Of course not!" said another girl fairy as she joined the growing crowd. "She would not for herself be looking!" In a matter of moments dozens of tiny girls and boys were hovering in front of Emma, squabbling with each other. Emma watched them, confused.

"Stop, everyone," Emma said, but no one paid any attention to her. "Please, where am I?"

The fairies kept on talking over her. Emma tried once more. "I said, STOP!"

The chattering stopped at once.

"Would someone please tell me where I am?" Emma said. The young fairy boy again flew up and bowed in front of her.

"Welcome to £areä," he said. At the mention of the place, Emma noticed that, for just a moment, the fairies bowed their heads.

"It's the land of the fairies," the young fairy boy added.

"Stupid she is not," said the girl fairy. "Her eyes see that we are fairies." Once again the fairies erupted into a squabbling chaos, only to be silenced when the golden fairy let out an ear-piercing whistle. Even Emma winced at the high sound.

"Ok," Emma said, taking the information in slowly, "and how did I get here?"

"Through the portal, of course," the golden fairy said, her arms folded.

"The portal?" Emma said. "What is that?"

All of the fairies rushed to answer at once.

"The lights…"

"….the big stone…"

"…glowing…"

Suddenly Emma remembered. Memories of the terrifying ride through the forest came flooding back, reminding her of the need to escape in the first place. The deadly mist was haunting her thoughts.

"By the shape-shifters you were being chased," the young boy fairy said, and then whispered, "Nice they are not." His fellow fairies nodded in agreement.

"Yeah," Emma said, "I got that feeling…when they almost strangled me." She thought for a moment. "How did you know the…shape-shifters were after me?"

"A distress call we received," the golden fairy said. "When we arrived, in distress you were."

"But I didn't call," Emma said.

"Oh, but you did," the golden fairy said. "However, in the forest you were *not* meant to be." Emma winced at the authoritative tone.

"Ok," Emma said, "but…why me? Why were they after me?"

"No more information we have," the golden fairy said impatiently. "Your questions the High Councilor must answer. But first, we must take care of…*this.*" The emphasis on the last word did not elude Emma, nor did the disapproving look the golden fairy gave as she glanced up and down at Emma's appearance.

For the first time since she had regained consciousness, Emma looked at her own hands. They were covered in a black sooty substance that extended up onto her arms. The upper extremities were not the only victims of the soot; her legs and feet had also fallen prey to the mysterious substance. Even though there wasn't a mirror in sight, Emma was pretty sure that the acrid smelling ash could be found on her face and in her hair as well.

"Not appropriate your appearance is," the golden fairy stated matter-of-factly. Emma's eyed narrowed as she silently questioned the fairy's harsh directive.

"Very close to getting you the shape-shifters were," the young boy fairy said.

"In the past that is now," the golden fairy said. "The present we must focus on." Turning to Emma, she asked, "Can you walk?" Emma nodded, and slowly stood.

"Far from here it is not. The best place it is, to take care of your...situation," the golden fairy explained as the other fairies took flight.

Emma took a step, but was stopped as the dizziness suddenly hit her. She crumpled to the ground and lay still, focusing only on her breathing.

The golden fairy flew close to her, studying her. "Worse it is than I thought. The shape-shifters had a tight grasp on you. Energy you do not have. To the pool we must get you—and quickly." She instructed the other fairies to gently lift Emma and carry her.

As the fairies flew, Emma took in the setting. They were in a clearing on the edge of a forest. The scene reminded Emma of a midwestern prairie— different colored flora dotted the open landscape, softly swaying back and forth in the light breeze. The flowers looked like a patchwork quilt, each hue taking on its own square. The fragrance from the blossoms filled the air with sweet smells of lovely summer afternoons.

The forest, on the other hand, was nothing like Emma had ever seen before. The trees filling the forest were large in size and stature—unusually large. Emma tried to catch a glimpse of the treetops, but to no avail. The trees looked coniferous in nature, but the needles sparkled in the filtered sunlight.

Guided by the dozens of fairies gently carrying her, Emma traveled for several minutes until she came to a natural rock bridge that rose out of the ground. The rock emitted a reddish glow, reminding Emma of the red clay mountains near her maternal grandparents' home in Utah.

"Under the bridge we must go," the golden fairy said to the others. "To the middle of the stone path. Leave the girl in the middle of the round stone." The fairies followed the directions, carefully carrying Emma under the rock landmark and down a narrow pathway. Water on both sides of the pathway churned in no particular pattern. As soon as Emma was placed upright on the round stone, the fairies flew away. Emma looked around her surroundings. She noticed that the carved structure she was now on held strange and unusual markings, similar to signs and symbols of ancient civilizations.

Suddenly, the water began to sparkle. Deep within the spring, bubbles formed and, when they broke the surface of the water, they shot straight up, creating a moving cyclone around Emma. She jumped at first, scared by the sudden burst. The water didn't touch her, but the mist began to work its magic on the blackened ash covering her body. Streams of black water ran off her arms and her legs, disappearing into the spring. Emma's face and hair once again took on a natural color as the silky mist caressed her skin. As the darkness of the soot disappeared, Emma felt a renewed alertness. The washing process ended with a burst of power like the steam on an old fashioned train. And then the spray was gone.

The fairies quickly surrounded Emma. They began to flutter around her, creating a gust of wind that gently dried her wet skin and hair. Minutes later the cleansing session was done. Emma leaned over the edge and looked at her reflection in the water. Her face was clean, her hands back to normal. There was not a speck of black ash to be found. There was only one problem—her hair. It seemed like each and every strand was sticking out straight from her scalp. She looked as if she had just put her finger into a light socket.

This is worse than humidity, Emma sighed. The fairies around her giggled and began taming each strand, wrapping it around other strands. Within minutes the unruly locks were controlled, pinned at her nape with a bright fuchsia flower.

"Hmmm, much better," the golden fairy said. "Now it is time to see the High Councilor." She turned and flew ahead of Emma, guiding the group out the other side of the stone path through a carved tunnel. Though darkness greeted them at the entrance,

Emma, strangely, wasn't scared. She followed the fairies inside.

Once her eyes adjusted, Emma realized that the tunnel wasn't completely dark. The fairies danced in the coolness of the cavern. Their wings illuminated the pathway, filling the darkness with a soft glow. As they quietly chatted with each other, their whispers echoed on the stone walls. Emma took in the pure beauty of the scene around her. Even though she was in a tunnel, the soft light gave off a warmth that shimmered in the air. For the first time since the shape-shifters had attacked her, she felt safe. For some time the group traveled through the underground pathway.

"We are here," the golden fairy announced. She pointed to a separate tunnel that ascended. At the top was a faint glow of light. "Go through there, you must. Alone."

"How will I know what to do?" Emma said. The fairies were already retreating through the cavern, the lights from their wings a distant glimmer.

"You will know." The whisper was spoken so clearly, Emma was sure that there was someone right behind her. She whipped around, only to realize that she was alone. She took a deep breath, turned, and walked into the tunnel. The light grew brighter and brighter as she made her way up to an opening.

As Emma emerged from the tunnel, she was blinded by the brightness. She squinted, trying to shield her eyes from the rays. A thought suddenly appeared in her mind.

Welcome, Emma.

Emma stopped abruptly. She waited for more—anything, but it didn't come. As her eyes slowly adjusted, she realized that she stood next to a rippling stream. Overhead the trees provided coverage from the sunlight. The sounds of the forest were nearby, but as far as she could tell, she was alone. She looked around her, but did not discover the source of the salutation.

"Hello?" Emma said.

Here.

The words melted into her mind like butter soaking into a warm dinner roll. Emma looked up. It took a moment to realize that the words belonged to a fairy, a young man. He slowly descended from a branch above to be at eye level with her.

Emma gasped. Her eyes grew wide as they focused on the intricate crown sitting on top of the fairy's reddish curls, an object that looked eerily familiar.

━┼ ┼━

The boy follows the fireflies to a city in the trees. There live the fairies. (Yes, I know—fairies. It isn't my choice for the story, but that's what happened in the dream.) The boy is pretty excited by all the fairies. They have a special party in his honor. There are lots of flowers (I guess fairies like flowers), music, and food. When it gets dark, the fireflies take over and light up the city in the trees…

I can't think up anything else to write.

--JPC

CHAPTER SIX

"Who are you?" Emma was surprised that her own voice broke the silence as the young fairy descended.

"I am the High Councilor," the fairy said. "For you I am Del." Del was dressed in a white gown and robe. As it softly swayed back and forth in the light wind, Emma noticed that it shimmered. His face, although young, carried wrinkles of worry or dissatisfaction. Emma couldn't tell which.

"Many questions I am sure you have," Del said as he turned and started to flutter in the air. "Come, and I will answer them." He led her to a tall tree, so tall that she couldn't see the top when she leaned back. A thick vine was wrapped around the tree. When Del touched it, it magically began to move and untangled itself, resting in front of Emma.

"Grab hold of the vine," Del instructed. Emma wrapped her hands and legs around the vine, and the vine began to move. Slowly Emma was carried up into the trees. Del moved silently next to her.

Emma was amazed. As they got higher and higher, she began to notice small houses hidden in the foliage. Some of the houses were carved right into the trunk of the tree itself, their shapes barely noticeable had it not been for small doors announcing the abodes. Other houses rested on branches, carefully hidden within the leaves. Intricate details were etched into the side of the houses, similar to the markings carved on the large washing stone. Fairies began to appear, and a soft chatter filled the treetops.

"The Castle of the Trees welcomes you," Del said as he waved his hands out in introduction. Emma took in the sight before her. Although she had never been to a rain forest, this is what she imagined the canopy to be like. Lush, green foliage filled every inch, allowing just enough sunlight in to create a soft glow that covered the area. Beautiful flora was everywhere—on fairy houses, dangling from branches, decorating flowing strands of fairy hair.

The moving vine seemed to know where to take Emma, for it climbed a bit higher and then wrapped itself around part of a nearby tree, giving Emma enough room to climb off. Emma maneuvered herself so that she was standing on a thick branch. As she looked beyond the tree she was standing on, she saw that the canopy of this forest was woven with branches. She could easily walk for miles in the canopy, moving from branch to branch.

"Food and drink to refresh ourselves, we must have first," Del said as he led the way from one branch to another. In the middle of the canopy was an open space where the branches had interlocked in a circle. In the space was a wooden platform, a balcony high in the trees. Fairies were meeting with others, reclining in the shade.

"We use this as our meeting ground," Del explained. "Fairies cannot fly for always. Flying takes much energy from us. To rest and renew, even we must do." Del pointed to a thick, stable branch off to the side. "To your liking this should be."

Emma hoisted herself onto the branch and sat down. No sooner had she gotten settled than fairies began to flutter around her, carrying bunches of grapes, strawberries—even a fruit she didn't recognize—and silently dropped them in her open palms, curtseying slightly before flying away. Two other fairies carried a pitcher of a sparkling green liquid, pouring it into a tall cylinder next to her.

"Eat first, and then, when we have renewed energy, we shall talk," Del said. Emma didn't need to be told twice. She didn't realize how hungry she was until the first bite. The green liquid provided a renewed sense of calmness that flowed through her body. As they ate, fairies around them sang softly, melodious tunes filling the air. Not even in her dreams could Emma envision a place more beautiful, a sense of peace more transparent.

The meeting ground was soon filled with fairies, gently flying from one branch to another. It appeared the fairies had recruited the help of the fireflies, because many had stayed around, their lights hidden here and there in the crooks of branches or on top of a leaf. It was just enough to melt the darkness away and replace it with a warm glow. Small fairies (perhaps children) wove brightly colored flowers together and carried them from branch to branch, reminding Emma of the garland on a Christmas tree. Another group of fairies carried large baskets of petals to the tops of the trees. When they reached the top, they turned the baskets upside-down, sending the petals gently floating in the air. When the petals reached the open meeting area, they froze in the air, slowly twirling back and forth, a shimmering reflection against the faint light of the fireflies.

Flower confetti, Emma thought to herself. Del laughed.

"Yes, our version of a celebration it is," he said. "We celebrate when a human enters our land. We have only had this happen once before."

"It's...beautiful," Emma whispered, not wanting to disturb the sight before her. The lights, the flowers, the fairies, the movement, the music filled her mind and her soul with such serenity, she didn't want it to end. She felt a tiredness overcoming her, and she leaned back against the trunk of the tree. Her eyelids became heavy, and even though she fought it, she couldn't ward off the sleep that was to come. Del touched the tree branch. It widened at the vertex of the trunk, large enough for Emma to lay down. Fairies gathered around her and gently carried her to the tree bed. A soft coverlet made of intertwining leaves was placed over her. She did not open her eyes.

"Sleep well, Emma," Del said. "Tomorrow all will be made known."

＝≼┼≽＝

The boy doesn't want the party to end, but it does. He sleeps for a long time. When he wakes up, there is a fairy ready to talk with him. The fairy introduces himself as the High Councilor. (I think the High Councilor is sort of like a mayor, but with a better sounding name.) Anyways, the High Councilor talks with the boy, and they walk on the branches in the forest. Fairies come out of their houses and welcome the boy. Their voices remind him of wind chimes.

--JPC

CHAPTER SEVEN

"Questions you have, and they are many," Del said as the last bits of food were eaten. Emma nodded her head in confirmation. She had awoken in her tree bed only minutes before to find Del sitting on a branch nearby, waiting for her. "The first being why you are here. I will answer all of your questions, but a story I must begin with. This will help you to understand our people." He ascended to a branch at eye level, and sat down.

"I am the High Councilor of these people. It is my duty to decide what is best. It is a difficult job. It is a serious job. Burdens every day I have of my great task, a task that has been placed upon me. A task that I was not meant to have."

The pain on Del's face did not escape Emma's notice.

"You see, to be High Councilor, chosen I was not," Del stopped for just a moment, looking off in the distance. "My father, the High Councilor before me, had selected another fairy, Lily, to take his place." Del stopped for a moment and looked at Emma. "In tune with others Lily always was. Finding value she did in spending time with our community. The High Councilor did value this skill. This trait he did see as wise. A problem there was, though. Lily did not want the job."

"Why not?" Emma asked.

"Confining it was for her," Del explained. "She was of an adventurous spirit—sometimes too adventurous. To choose her own life path she wanted."

Del stopped again and looked out over the Castle. Fairies were moving from house to house, whispering in small groups, playing with each other. Del smiled and looked at Emma.

"I look at our community. A smile it creates," he said. "I see what we have—a sense of belonging, of order. Hard work has brought us this over many years. Yet, she would not have been happy, I know." Again, the shadows crossed his face. Emma knew the shadows well; they always appeared when her mother missed her father.

"So, what happened to her?" Emma asked.

"One day into the forest she left to play—'The Forbidden Zone' as my father called it. Scary stories he would warn us with, but Lily didn't believe him. She left. I went along—not to play, but to guard her I did.

"In the forest we were. Everything was fine. Suddenly, captured in a net Lily was by humans. The net was too heavy. Entangled were her wings. She couldn't escape. Then, they ripped off her wing. To the ground she was thrown."

"How horrible!" Emma cried. "How could they do that?"

Del shook his head. "I waited until they left. To her I called and called, but she did not answer. She just laid there in the forest. Dead I thought she was. Then, another human came. Different, he was. He was...kind. With care he picked her up."

"And you never saw her again?" Emma said.

"No, I did see her. For some time," Del said. "To a house the human took her. I would visit every day. He fed her special food, and her wound bandaged. Slowly she began to heal. That was when I realized that she had changed."

"Changed?" Emma said. "How?"

"At first, she knew I was near," Del said. "Look for me, she would, although I am not sure she saw me. Then, one day...she stopped looking. Her decision she had made."

"Decision? What decision?" Emma said.

Del sighed. "Emma, a choice all creatures of the forest have—to stay with their communities or to leave for another land. Only once is the decision made. Almost all stay within their own communities, perhaps from a sense of loyalty. Well, almost all."

Emma sensed from Del's tone and his downcast eyes that Lily's choice had brought pain to the inhabitants of £areä. Del explained to her what it had been like to realize that Lily wasn't coming back to the land of the fairies. He described how he had returned and told his father, the High Councilor, what had happened. The old fairy had taken ill not long afterward, and had never recovered. Del suspected that he had died of a broken heart.

"Why did Lily choose to leave?" Emma said. Del sighed.

"The reason was one only. Love," he said. "Something that we fairies cannot understand nor obtain. Love she had found." Even though sadness filled the air, a faint smile formed on Del's face.

"So, if Lily chose to live in the land of the humans, she could never return to £areä?" Emma asked.

"No," Del answered, "Dangerous it would be for her, and for us as well. Other creatures are constantly seeking a way into our portal, only to defeat our kingdom. At risk everyone would be if Lily tried to come back. Plus, when a creature chooses to cross over into another land, there are consequences. A different form the creature takes. Forever. Lily became human, therefore."

"Wait." Emma's brain was working faster than her voice. "How was Lily able to even go through the portal to begin with? The golden fairy told me that she was only allowed to go into the forest for a distress call."

"Kia—fairy of gold, as you say—is correct. Somewhat," Del said. "When fairies sense distress, they are allowed to go through the portal, but hurry they must. The journey is timed and, after a certain passage of time, the portal is closed. Lost forever are fairies still in the forest." Emma shivered at the thought of being lost forever. Del continued.

"Another way through the portal there is—a special ability," Del said. He pointed to the crown sitting on his head. "Only a fairy royal has the ability to travel through the portal without time limits. The royals are bound to the crown—for travel, both royal blood and the crown are needed. While the crown offers untimed passage, a target it is for other creatures who want to gain access as well. Other creatures hunt the crown. Some say they can even smell it."

For a moment Emma took in everything that Del had said. As she processed his words, something in her mind clicked. She then reached into her jeans pocket and pulled out the small crown. She held it in her outstretched hand. The soft rays of sunlight hit the ring and caused it to glow.

"You mean…this is a crown?" Emma said. Del nodded. "Is this why I was being chased in the forest?"

Del nodded again. "Convinced I am that the shape-shifters smelled the crown. If they would have obtained the crown, they would have entered our world and destroyed it. For this reason the fairies rescued you and brought you here."

Emma's head was swimming with all the information that had been presented to her. Del could tell that she was having a difficult time sorting through things. He spoke up.

"Emma," Del said. "Not for entertainment is the purpose of this story. This story tells you about our land, our people, and even me."

"If Lily was royalty, then you must be royalty, too," Emma said. Del nodded.

"Yes," Del said. "Lily was my sister."

"I still don't understand what this has to do with me, though," Emma sighed. "You said that royalty and the crown must go together. I am not royalty."

"But you are, Emma," Del said. "This story I told you so you could also understand *you*. After all, you know Lily." Emma's head swung around to look at Del.

"What?"

"Lily, you know. Think, Emma," Del said slowly.

Emma did think. Surely she didn't know anyone resembling a fairy, or even anyone who might have left a land long ago. It would have been someone that seemed a bit out of place. After all, being human wasn't a natural thing. Perhaps the person would struggle with social skills—what was or was not appropriate at certain times or even how to act in certain situations. Maybe this person still had a longing to be close to nature...

Emma's eyes grew wide. She gasped. She knew.

Lily. Lila.

Grams.

The High Councilor is…well, I guess the best word to describe him is that he's nice. He's kind. He's patient. The boy can see that the other fairies respect the High Councilor by how they give him space. When the High Councilor is with the boy, it's familiar—like they are friends. (Don't ask me how…I don't know. I am just writing a fiction story, remember?) Most of all, the boy feels safe when he's with the High Councilor. So the High Councilor starts the story…

I'm going to have to write about that later. Dinner's calling.

--JPC

CHAPTER EIGHT

Del was quiet for some time. He allowed Emma to take in the fact that she had just realized.

Grams, at one time, had been a fairy. The thought sunk in. And Emma began with the questions.

"Did my grandpa—Gramps—know that she was…you know, a fairy?" Emma said.

"Yes," Del said. "He was the love she found."

Of course, it made sense, thought Emma to herself. Gramps was the boy who found the injured fairy in the forest. He was the caring teenager who rescued her, nursing her back to health, although she would never be the same. She could never go back again, not after she had found him. Not after she had found love.

"And my dad?" Emma managed to say the words with a slight twinge of pain. "Did he know about Grams, too?"

Del shook his head. "That I do not know, Emma. The connection between Lily and our world had dissolved by that time. I wish I had been able to hold on, but…" Again, sadness hung in the air. Emma waited for a moment, and then broke the melancholy feeling.

"I think he was here," Emma said quietly. "I read about…this place. In his journal." She waited for Del to object, but he did not.

"Yes, here he was," Del said. "He was young in your human years, I think, and he made his way here. Surprised we were when the fireflies brought him to us."

"Why did he never say anything about this?" Emma asked.

Del shook his head. "Perhaps the same thing that happened to Lily happened to him. Forget they slowly did." Emma nodded quietly. It made sense, especially since her father's journal felt more like a story than a memoir.

Emma could never imagine forgetting a place like this. How sad to experience something so magical—so surreal—only to have the memory of it fade away.

"I don't think Grams has forgotten this place," Emma said. "Maybe somewhat, but not entirely." She told Del about the garden, and the many flowers that Grams tended to daily. She mentioned the birdhouses and the wind chimes, both reminders of a land lost.

"She brought a piece of £areä with her," Emma said. "She likes to spend a lot of time in her garden, I think, because it is comforting. She was just telling me about flowers—what are those names again? I'm not very good with flowers, or basically anything living. Peony, Rose, Del...dolphin..."

"Delphinium," Del said quietly.

"Yes!" Emma said. "How did you know...?" She looked at Del for a moment and then realized. "Delphinium, Del. You are named after a flower, aren't you?"

"All we are," Del waved his hands to the other fairies nearby. "Corea for coreopsis, Salvia..."

"For Sal," Emma said.

"Rose—well, easy that is," Del added.

"And Kia?" Emma asked.

"Rubeckia," Del said. Emma gave him a blank look, not understanding. "'Black-eyed Susans' you humans call them. A peaceful name like 'rubeckia,' we prefer. For now, enough about our names. Your purpose we must talk about."

"I am here because of the crown, aren't I?" Emma said. "Oh, and because I am part royalty, with Grams being a former fairy and all."

"No, Emma. A role you have, a task you must do," Del said. "It starts with saving your grandmother."

"What? What has happened to Grams?" Emma jumped up. "Is she hurt?"

"To the edge of the forest Lily followed you. The shape-shifters sensed her, but already had you in their grip. They attacked her, and she was knocked unconscious."

"And you waited all this time to tell me this?" Emma moved toward the vine. "I have to help her. I have to leave now!" She wrapped her arms around the vine, waiting for it to move, but it didn't budge.

"And how will you help her? How will you get to her?" Del said.

"I have the crown," Emma said. "And I am royalty. You said that both are needed to leave. I can leave."

"On the other side the shape-shifters are waiting for you," Del said. "They know you are here. Waiting they are until you enter the forest again. How will you escape from them?" Emma's arms went limp and she turned toward Del.

"I…I don't know." The memory of the shape-shifters surrounding her, their misty tentacles closing in on her throat, sent shivers throughout her.

Del was right. She wouldn't be able to escape them again.

"Then what do I do?" Emma said.

"The crown must be destroyed," Del said.

"Can't we just throw it away somewhere—like in a big lake?" Emma said.

"No, danger there is that other creatures from other lands will find it," Del said. "In order to truly make our land safe—and save your grandmother— destroyed the crown must be, and this must be done by you."

"Me?!" Emma said. "I can't do it. I don't know how to do it."

"A prophecy there is. An ancient fairy rime was written about this time," Del said. "It was written for the one who save the fairies would:

A constant darkness shadows thee,
time overlaps and intertwines,
fear and doubt,
swirling
Death creeps up,
uninviting
A creature like no other enters
And steps into the unknown, not seeing what she
feels
Who reaches against all belief
That which accepts what has been given as good

And in turn,
Gives all for all given
will overcome the darkness."

Del looked at Emma. "This prophecy is about you. The hope you are."

Emma laughed. "This isn't about me. I'm only fourteen."

"You are the hope," Del said again.

"This can't be about me," Emma argued, panic rising.

"It is about you, Emma," Del said.

"I don't have special skills," Emma said, walking in place. "I don't know what to do. How do I destroy the crown? How do I save Grams? How do I make it back without being taken by the shape-shifters again? How?" Emma cried, tears pooling in her eyes.

"I know how, Emma," Del's voice was soft and tranquil, soothing and calming her fears. He stood silently as she paced back and forth, watching her work through her thoughts. Finally she stopped and looked at him.

Emma sighed slowly. She wiped her eyes and looked at Del.

"There is no other way around this, is there?" she asked. He shook his head.

"You are the only hope," he said. "You it must be."

Emma took a deep breath.
"I know that now. Tell me what to do."
And he did.

✄⊹⊹➤

The story the High Councilor tells goes something like this:

There once was this fairy with red hair. She liked to play in the woods, even though her dad didn't really like it. (I think dads don't like it when their kids have fun.) Anyways, she had trouble one day because these boys picked on her. Actually, they broke one of her wings. Not a good thing for a fairy, because everybody knows that a fairy needs its wings to fly.

So, the fairy is left on the ground. But this other boy comes by and decides to help her. He takes her to his home and helps her get better. She misses her family, but she and the boy become good friends. She finally decides to stay with the boy. When she makes this decision, she gives up ever going back to see her family again…

The High Councilor is sad.

---JPC

CHAPTER NINE

Find the three, and the fourth will find you.

Those were the words Del had spoken right before Emma had left the fairy commune. He had told her of the journey she had to travel in search of the three things she would need to defeat the shape-shifters. To her disappointment, he hadn't told her *what* three things she would be looking for.

"When you see it, you will know," a voice beside her said. Emma jumped. She still wasn't used to the mind-reading abilities that all fairies seemed to have. She turned and came face-to-face with Kia. She groaned silently and rolled her eyes.

"Do not think that I welcome this arrangement any more than you do," Kia said. "This journey I did not ask for." Kia was right. Neither of them had wanted to go on a journey, let alone with each other. Emma had resigned herself to the fact that she alone was Grams' only hope for survival. She had accepted the fact that she must be the one to sacrifice the crown. Even when Del explained to her that she would have to find specific things to help her in this challenge—things stated in the ancient rime of the fairies—she was willing to go ahead. It was only when Del insisted that Emma have a traveling partner, and that the partner would be Kia, that Emma disagreed. Emma was independent. She could handle things on her own or, at least, she thought so. She especially didn't want to have Kia as a traveling companion.

No matter what strategy she tried in her debate, Del came back with an even stronger argument, until finally, Emma gave in. Emma and Kia had left the commune in silence. Silence until now.

"I didn't ask for this either," Emma said, "but apparently this is the only way to save your people, and Grams. Unless, of course, you have a better idea." Kia remained silent. Good, Emma thought to herself. At least it's quiet again.

The pair wandered through the forest for some time. They came to a meadow full of flowers. The flowers, mostly blue and purple hues, swayed in the light breeze, their tall spikes waving at Kia and Emma as they passed by.

"Wait," Kia called out as she stopped midair. She looked around, searching for something.

"What?" Emma said, agitated. She only wanted to get to their destination, find the three objects, destroy the crown, and go back home. Emma was not in the mood for side trips.

"These flowers," Kia said, flying from one flower to the next. "These are lavenias, a type of flower that offers healing and strength. For later we might need them." She began to pick the flowers and gather them in her arms. Emma watched.

"Stand there, do not," Kia said. "Put these in your bag." She handed the flowers to Emma, and Emma brought them to her nose. They offered a light, delicate smell. She dropped them in the hand-woven shoulder bag Del had given her for the journey. She fingered the outside of the bag. The fairies had made it out of plant stems, carefully interlocking each blade together. It was sturdy and would hold all necessary supplies for the trip. Plus, it would free her hands for any necessary tasks.

Kia led the way out of the meadow into another part of the forest. The trees filtered the sunlight as they traveled deeper and deeper into the woods. Emma decided to attempt a conversation.

"So, how did you know about the flowers?" she asked. "That they're...good, and all?"

"About flowers all fairies know," Kia said, not bothering to look at Emma. "It is our business." Emma realized this was true. Grams knew a lot about flowers. Just looking at her garden, one could tell that flowers were her business, her way of life. Fairies found comfort in flowers; Emma was sure that Grams did as well.

"What will we need the flowers for?" Emma asked.

"The journey ahead I do not know," Kia shook her head. "Prepared it is best to be." Emma wanted to ask what they needed to prepare for, but she could tell from Kia's determined brow that the conversation was done.

They walked on in silence. The tree branches gently moved in the breeze that slowly danced through the forest. Soft rays of sunlight descended from the tops of the trees down to the forest floor. In almost all aspects, Emma could easily close her eyes and pretend that she was back in her world, back at Gram's house.

The only difference was the sound. Back in her world—at Gram's house—the familiar sounds of cicadas or grasshoppers or chirping birds would fill the air. It was a sound that she came to recognize, and long for. Those sounds were not here.

Instead, the sounds were different. Emma could only explain it as if everything had a sound—the gentle breeze sounded like a whisper, a flower blooming might sound like a soft yawn. Even Kia's wings carried the sound of muffled fluttering.

The sounds were distinct and foreign to Emma's ears. It was difficult for her to truly experience £areä. In many regards, she felt like she was looking down on herself inside this fantastical world. She strained to listen for more sounds—anything familiar.

And then she heard it.

Water.

"Kia, I hear water. There's water nearby!" Emma said. She listened again, trying to locate where the sound was coming from. Then she took off.

"Emma, wait!" Kia called out after her, but it was no use. Emma kept going through the woods until she reached the edge of a small pond. The rippling water was a translucent blue, undulating back and forth with the gentle breeze. Emma bent down and was about to put her hand in when Kia's voice stopped her.

"Emma, that I would not do," Kia warned.

"What?" Emma asked. "It's just water, and I want to see how cool it is." She turned back to the water, and looked down, noticing movement under the surface. A small fish was swimming in front of her, its scales reflecting various colors like a slowly turning kaleidoscope. To Emma, it appeared as though a rainbow was moving through the water. As she bent down to get a closer look, she dipped her hand below the water's surface.

Suddenly the fish jumped up, and as it broke the surface of the water, it changed. In a split second, it grew to a size drastically larger than Emma herself. The mouth opened, revealing jagged, sharp teeth positioned to devour its prey. Emma screamed and fell back, scrambling to get away. The giant fish fell back into the water, its shape returning to its original size.

Emma sat on the ground, trying to catch her breath. She glanced over at Kia, who was giggling.

"Why are you laughing?" Emma said, perturbed. "That…that thing could have killed me!"

"Kill you, it would not," Kia said in between chuckles. "It is a magic fish. Harmless it is."

"Harmless?!" Emma said, sitting up. "Did you see the teeth? It was bigger than me!"

"Be assured that it means no harm," Kia said. "It was simply unnerved that you had entered its territory. The water its home is."

"Why is it even in £areä?" Emma asked. "I thought this was the home of the fairies." Kia flew ahead and then sat down on a branch, contemplating Emma's question.

"£areä is the home of the fairies," she began, "but, over time, loyal many friends have been.

Shelter from other dangers they need. They live in peace in £areä."

"You mean, there are other…creatures here besides just fairies?"

Kia nodded. Emma thought for a moment.

"But I'm…we're not in danger, right?" Again Kia nodded. Silently, Emma let out a sigh of relief. She wasn't in a hurry to experience the same feeling the shape-shifters brought when they tried to suffocate her.

For some time Emma sat at the water's edge, watching the lone magic fish slowly swim around. Soon, other magic fish joined the scene. The school of fish moved under the water, creating ripples of color beneath the surface of the small lake. Although she wasn't completely trusting of them just yet, she had to admit that they were beautiful to see.

"Go we must," Kia said, breaking the stillness. "Traveling we still must do." Emma nodded and stood up. She glanced back one last time at the magic fish swimming under the clear water, and then turned to follow Kia.

The two travelers followed a narrow forest path for some time in silence. Enveloped in her own thoughts, Emma couldn't help but realize how much had happened in the last day. Her mother had dropped her off at Grams' house, believing it would be a quiet weekend. It had been anything but a quiet weekend! She had found the hidden items in the attic, traveled through the portal, been welcomed by the residents of £areä, and had accepted the challenge of saving not only the fairies of £areä, but also Grams herself. If she wasn't living out the journey herself, she realized that she would have a hard time believing it.

"Here, we are," Kia announced.

Emma looked around. They had entered an open area on the edge of the forest. The clearing was the opposite of the warm, inviting forest they had just left. The dark, charcoal colored rocks that existed everywhere she looked were jagged and let off a cold, permeating mist. Emma could see that, in the distance, the clearing stopped. She walked to the edge and looked out. A large abyss swallowed all light below. Across the abyss loomed a black mountain.

"There," Kia said, pointing to the summit of the mountain across the abyss. "We must go there."

"How do you know?" Emma asked.

"Del left me with some parting instructions," Kia said. "To point you in the right direction of the destination is my job. That is where 'the fourth will find you.'"

"Well, that is great and all," Emma said, "but exactly how are we supposed to get there? I am seeing nothing but a big drop below, and high cliffs ahead."

"A problem-solver I am not," Kia said. "Del simply asked me to guide you. Some of the work you must do yourself, you know."

Emma huffed and walked away. Great, she thought to herself. I am being disciplined by a fairy. This is worse than staying at Grams' house. For a moment Emma felt a twinge in her heart. As she looked around her at the dark mountain, the deep cliffs, and the black unknown, being at Grams' house seemed almost welcoming.

I know I have a job to do, Emma thought. But how do I do it? How can we possibly get across this chasm? She shook her head in despair.

"Kia," Emma called out to the fairy on the opposite side of the clearing. "Can't you just fly over to the other side? Isn't that what fairies do?"

It was Kia's turn to huff. "No, 'fly over to the other side' I cannot. The journey is too long, even for me. Plus, my instructions were to not leave you." More silence followed. Emma turned and focused on the expanse before her.

She who steps into the unknown.

What unknown? Emma thought to herself. There isn't anything there. She sighed and closed her eyes, resting her head in her hands. That's when she saw it.

Slowly a narrow bridge began to form in front of her, leading from one side of the chasm to the other side. Emma opened her eyes, and the bridge disappeared. She walked to the edge of the cliff and closed her eyes again. The bridge slowly formed again, gently swaying like a pendulum in slow motion.

Can it really be as easy as this? She thought to herself.

She who steps into the unknown.

With her eyes still closed and the vision of the bridge in front of her, Emma cautiously put her left foot out. In her mind she saw her foot connect with the flatness of the bridge walkway. Slowly she began to feel the hard surface beneath her shoe. She moved her right foot into place as well. Slowly she ventured, checking her balance. Her hands reached out to steady herself, and instantly she felt the hardness of guardrails. Her feet inched forward, making progress along the invisible bridge. Emma felt a flutter next to her. Kia had landed on her shoulder.

"Isn't this amazing, Kia?" Emma said as she turned to look at Kia.

"No, Emma!" Kia exclaimed. "Do not open your eyes! Do not look!"

But it was too late.

K. R. Burg

The High Councilor tells the boy that there is danger outside of the land of the fairies. Creatures want to hurt the fairies. The High Councilor explains that there is a poem—a special message—that explains someone will come and help them. The boy is scared, but the fairies tell him he is safe...

---JPC

CHAPTER TEN

The next three seconds were the most crucial of Emma's life.

In the first second, Emma realized her catastrophic mistake instantly. Her eyes had been closed, and the bridge had existed. In a split second, however, she had become distracted and opened her eyes—and the bridge had vanished. Adrenalin sparked deep inside her, sending warning signals to her brain. She frantically reached out to grasp something—anything. There was nothing now, nothing separating her from the black abyss below.

The next second brought on a surge of heightened awareness. Emma was in full panic mode, her eyes wide with fright and her body tilted backward in a falling motion. She looked up, her hands reaching out, her mouth wide open to scream. Yet, no sound came.

It was the third second that stopped all sound, all motion. Emma stood frozen, not daring to look around her for fear that the momentum would start again. In her periphery she could barely see Kia above her.

"Emma," Kia breathed heavily. "Hurry! The bridge you must bring back."

Emma turned her head slightly. What she saw made her gasp. Kia was suspended in space. Her wings were frozen in flight, not moving. Strands of coal black hair extended out in all directions. Kia's dark eyes were determined, her brow furrowed. It was Kia's hands that caught Emma's attention.

Each hand held a wave of undulating light that circled Emma and joined on the other side. Kia's spread fingers held thousands of tiny glowing strands, separated within the gently moving wave, filling the space within so that a sphere of moving light formed around Emma.

"Emma," Kia said again. "You can move now. Safe it is." Kia's words were muffled by the beating of Emma's own heart. The determined fairy continued to hover above as Emma slowly righted herself. She glanced at the abyss below. It was still there, its mist frozen in mid-churn.

"The bridge," Kia instructed. "The bridge you must focus on."

Emma closed her eyes and thought of the bridge, but nothing appeared.

"I…I can't," Emma stammered. "It's not working."

"You have to," Kia breathed. "More strength I do not have."

Emma closed her eyes again. Nothing. No bridge, no guardrails, nothing. Tears welled up in her eyes as she shook her head.

"It's no use!" she cried. "It's gone. I can't bring it back." She hid her eyes with her hands, a sob escaping her throat.

"Emma, please…" Kia whispered. Her strength was sifting through her fingers into the light waves. She couldn't hold on much longer.

What am I going to do? Emma thought to herself. I can't do this. This is too big for me.

She who steps into the unknown.

But I can't, Emma screamed in her mind. Tears flowed down her cheeks. I can't bring it back, she thought. I close my eyes, but it isn't there.

How do you know?

I can't see it, Emma stopped. It's not there because I can't see it.

Just because you can't see it doesn't mean it isn't there.

Emma stood up. She looked at Kia, who was struggling, pleading. Emma wiped her tears, and then closed her eyes. Again, no bridge came into focus.

That doesn't mean that you aren't here, Emma said to herself. You are here. I know it. I felt it. I just have to find you.

With her eyes open, she slowly put her left foot out, searching for a foundation beneath. At first, nothing came. Emma moved her foot around, searching, searching. The sensation of a hard surface beneath slowly formed, working its way first through her toes, then her heel, through her ankle and then up her leg. She responded by inching her other foot in front, waiting for the feeling to come again. It did. She extended her hands out, curving her fingers as though she were holding onto guardrails. The empty feeling of air was replaced with the hard, cold feeling of metal. Emma exhaled.

"Kia, it's here," Emma said. "I can't see it, but I can feel it. I know the bridge is here."

"Emma, you must hold on," Kia said. "When I let go, past time will collide with present time. Pretty it is not."

"What about you?" Emma asked. "What are you going to do?"

Kia shook her head. "Worry about me, you will not, Emma. Hold on…now!"

Emma grasped the guardrails with all her strength as Kia's hands shot straight up, her fingers letting go of the light waves. A powerful force threw Emma against the guardrail, but she held on. The strong wave swept through the abyss, creating a violent wind echoing throughout. The force hit the side of the mountain and, turning back like a pendulum, collided with Emma a second time, although less powerfully. She managed to plant her feet and hands just in time as the force passed her and disappeared, leaving only silence.

Emma stood on the bridge, breathing heavily. She listened carefully, but the only sound she heard was her own intake of air. She cautiously loosened her grip on the guardrails one finger at a time.

"Kia?" Emma whispered. "Where are you?"

Silence.

"Kia?" Emma's heart began to beat rapidly again. The thought that she was all alone in this abyss, stranded on a bridge she couldn't see, in the midst of a quest she couldn't understand, was almost more than she could handle. Her rising panic was interrupted by a faint sound.

"Here am I," a whisper echoed.

"Where?" Emma asked, frantically looking all around her.

"The hood of your clothing, I am in," Kia said faintly. "I was thrown against you, and would have fallen in the abyss had it not been for this giant net."

Emma smiled and breathed again. "I can't see you. Are you alright?"

"In pain, I am," Kia responded. "But I will heal. To move us quickly is your job. Go."

Emma didn't wait for more detailed commands. She held onto the guardrails as though she were walking on a moving conveyor belt at the airport, her strides brisk, sure in the knowledge that there was a bridge beneath each step. She looked straight ahead at the mountain before her, her focus on the final destination. In a matter of minutes, they reached the edge of the mountain cliff and stepped off, collapsing at the entrance to a cave. Kia climbed out of the hood and lay on the ground, her chest rising and falling with each breath. Emma leaned against the side of the cave wall, her heartbeat slowing and her eyes heavy. The thought that they were both safe on the other side of the abyss comforted her as sleep overtook her.

━╬━

When the boy is with the fairies, he sees many things. He sees magic, but he doesn't really know that it is magic because it is…normal. The fairies take turns showing him their magic gifts. I will explain two of the gifts the boy sees:

One fairy flies up to the boy. Behind the fairy is a small animal—it looks sort of like a bunny. The fairy starts talking a strange language, and the bunny answers. (I am not making this up. Remember, this is a dream that I had. Crazy stuff happens in dreams, ok?) Anyways, the boy and the bunny talk together for many minutes.

Another fairy calls to the boy. He walks over to the fairy, but when he is almost by her, she disappears. He looks all around, and he can't find her. But he hears giggling—it sounds like wind chimes. Suddenly, she reappears in front of him. She was there the whole time, but the boy just couldn't see her.

Sometimes I think that I am invisible, too…

--JPC

CHAPTER ELEVEN

When Emma opened her eyes, she knew neither what time it was nor how long she had slept. What she did know was that she was hungry, which was a good thing, as Kia was quietly preparing an array of different foods. Emma watched her for some time, not wanting to disturb the scene. Finally, she spoke.

"That thing you did—on the bridge," Emma said, "the thing with the light? That was cool." Kia looked up briefly at Emma, and then continued her food preparation. Emma tried again to start a conversation.

"So, can all fairies do that?" she asked. Kia stopped and looked at Emma.

"No, not all fairies can do that," she said as she set the food aside. "All fairies have powers, but accordingly the High Councilor does choose. I was given the gift of time-bending."

"You can stop time?" Emma asked. Her mind struggled to understand this special power.

"Stopping time, I do not," Kia corrected. "Time I bend to slow down." Emma thought back to the experience on the bridge. It sure felt that they had been standing still in space, but to know that they were still moving even the slightest bit sent a shiver up Emma's spine. Nonetheless, Emma was impressed. There was more to Kia than she first realized. She was beginning to understand why Del insisted on this pint-sized traveling partner.

"Eat you must," Kia instructed Emma as she flew over and deposited a folded cloth in Emma's hands. Emma unfolded the cloth and found an offering of bite-size foods—pieces of bread, cheeses, fruits, and even nuts.

"Where did you get this?" Emma asked. "I didn't see a bag of food anywhere."

Kia smiled. "Fairies travel 'lightly.'" She pulled out a small vial of purple liquid, uncorked the top, and let one drop fall on her hand. Emma's eyes grew wide as the drop instantly began to grow into a bite-size piece of bread. Kia flew over and dropped the piece on Emma's food pile.

"People would love this 'magic cooking potion' in my world," Emma said, amazed. She saw visions of people scrambling to stores just to buy the purple vials. TV commercials would sell the liquid, claiming that it would bring families closer together, alleviating all problems of knowing what to cook for dinner, cutting grocery bills in half, and ending world hunger. The purple liquid craze would spin out of control.

"What is it like…in your world?" Kia asked. Emma raised an eyebrow, surprised that Kia was even interested in her life.

"Well," Emma started, "it's a lot like £areä…except without fairies." She stopped a moment to think about what to say next. "There are a lot of people—especially in the cities…"

"What is 'cities'?" Kia asked.

"Oh, a city is a place with a lot of buildings and cars and…" Emma could tell that Kia was already lost. She tried a different approach. "I guess my world has some things that are the same as yours—like trees and flowers. And peace. I think that there is a lot of peace in £areä, and there is in my world, too, but not always. There is fighting as well."

"Fighting there is in my world, too," Kia said. "Not in £areä, but just outside." Kia's words reminded Emma of the presence of evil when the shapeshifters were after her. Emma nodded in agreement.

"There are other things in my world—happiness, laughter, sadness…" Emma said.

"What is 'sadness'?" Kia asked.

Emma was quiet for a moment as she searched for an answer. How do you explain sadness? How do you explain when something so awful happens to you that you feel your heart has died inside? How do you explain that there aren't enough tears in the universe to show how you feel? How do you explain that there are days you don't want to go on, that it is a fight just to breathe because the one thing that held you together is gone, and isn't coming back?

Emma exhaled slowly. "Sadness is like…the sun dying, and leaving everything cold and dark." Kia took in Emma's words for some time. She finally broke the stillness.

"Sadness I do not like," she said quietly as her eyes met Emma's.

Neither do I, Emma thought.

The two travelers walked for some time along the ridge of the mountain pass, taking in the view. Before them loomed vast mountain peaks, charcoal gray in appearance only to be dabbed with specks of white near the summits. Although there was the presence of snow, the air held no tinge of coldness. The sky hung low with a thin layer of blue peeking out from drooping clouds.

Something had been bothering Emma for some time while they walked. Del had been adamant about Emma being the chosen one to save £areä, the fairies, and her grandmother. He had also explained the prophecy of the chosen one, the rime that foretold what would transpire. What confused Emma were Del's last words: *Find the three and the fourth will find you.* What three? Surely they had not just gone through the terror of the invisible bridge for nothing. There must have been something that they had to collect or receive from the experience, something that would help Emma in her ultimate quest against the shape-shifters. Perhaps Kia would know.

"Kia," she said. The fairy stopped a short ways ahead and turned back. "Del mentioned a prophecy about the chosen one. I understand that is me."

Kia nodded, but didn't say anything. Emma continued.

"What I don't understand is the connection with the prophecy and the things we need to find. When are we going to start looking for the items?"

Kia smiled. "Emma, one item you have already found."

"I have?" Emma asked, confused. "I didn't see anything."

"It is not what you see, but what you *gain*."

Emma thought back to the episode on the bridge. It had been terrifying, stepping out with her eyes closed. The fact that she could see the bridge in her mind was a reassurance. Yet, when she had made the mistake of opening her eyes, everything disappeared. Emma had to find the strength inside herself to step out onto a bridge that she *couldn't* see, but could only feel. A far more difficult task. She remembered how much her legs were shaking, how difficult it was to even find her balance.

"So the bridge was the first task," Emma said slowly. "And I discovered something. I was so scared…"

"As was I," Kia interrupted.

She who steps out into the unknown.

"I had to step out…" Emma said, and then it hit her. "Even when I couldn't see the bridge…"

She who steps out into the unknown.

"Even when I was scared…" Then Emma knew. "I had to have courage."

Kia smiled. "Courage you did have, a necessary tool. You will need courage to overcome the shape-shifters."

"But I was scared," Emma said.

"Emma, courage appears in the midst of fear," Kia said. "Courage defeats fear."

Emma let Kia's words slowly sink in. Prior to arriving in £areä, she had never defined herself as courageous. In fact, squeamish, afraid, and fearful were words that came to mind. And yet, she had stepped out, found the bridge again, and saved both Kia and herself. Perhaps courage was something that could be more than just a far off wish.

Emma stopped for a moment and looked around her. They had been walking for hours. The terrain had become rough and jagged, and she had to constantly check the path ahead so as not to trip over a large rock or lose her footing on a hidden crevice. The mountainous surface was barren, absent of any signs of life. How different these surroundings were compared with the Castle of the Trees, Emma thought to herself. When she was high in the trees, she felt safe and secure. The greenness surrounding the small abodes tucked into tree trunks and crooked branches pulsated with joy and life. The mountainous landscape Emma viewed all around her was void of feeling. She easily could have thought that she was the only living being in the world, standing on the top of the mountain ridge.

"Climb, we must," Kia said as she led the way to the mountain's edge. Emma followed, confused. They were on top of the mountain ridge, so climbing higher wasn't an option. Where were they going?

"Where are we climbing?" Emma asked.

"Down," Kia said as she flew over the edge and disappeared.

"You're joking, right?" Emma glanced over the edge and almost lost her breakfast. The brief scene provided a steep cliff, partially covered in dense fog.

"What is 'joking'?" Kia asked, reappearing.

"Never mind," Emma said. "Do we have ropes or something else to use?"

"Hands you have," Kia answered, again disappearing. "And courage."

"Hands and courage aren't going to help much when I slip and fall to my death," Emma mumbled.

"Everything I hear," Kia's voice floated back up to where Emma was still standing. "Now, climb."

Emma slowly crawled out to the ledge, exhaled slowly, and lowered herself over. Her hands and legs shook as she searched for rocks to grab onto. She didn't deny she was nervous; yet, she had learned from the invisible bridge scene the importance of staying in control. She quickly found footholds and, maneuvering herself sideways, located handholds as well. The charcoal-gray rock was an excellent surface to climb—not too slippery, not too rough. Emma learned quickly that climbing down a mountain was much harder than climbing up a mountain, mainly because the climber can't always see where he or she needs to go. Working steadily, she made slow progress down the side of the cliff. Kia flew around Emma, guiding her by pointing out nearby rocks that could be used as anchor points. When she was tired, Kia would perch on Emma's shoulder, content with the ride.

I can't believe I am climbing down the side of a cliff—and without a rope, Emma thought as she looked sideways for another foothold. She found one (with Kia's help) and carefully stepped. She realized that only twenty-four hours earlier she had been at Grams' house, dreading the weekend. How much had happened in twenty-four hours! A faint feeling of remorse surfaced as Emma thought about her own behavior. She had learned so much about Grams from the fairies already. She would never look at Grams the same way.

"Here we must go." Kia's words broke into Emma's thoughts. Emma looked to where Kia was pointing. A small tunnel no bigger than the size of a manhole on its side was half hidden by rocks. If Kia hadn't been pointing directly at the entrance, Emma would have missed it altogether. She leaned closer and looked in.

"Where does it lead?" Emma asked.

"To the center of the mountain it takes us," Kia explained. "A different route I would prefer, but this path has been chosen for us." Kia didn't elaborate, and although she was curious, Emma was too tired from the climb to ask. Kia flew to the opening, turned and looked at Emma, and then disappeared into the darkness. Emma scurried to the entrance and crouched down. She realized that the opening was too small to walk in. She would have to crawl.

As she slowly moved inside the tunnel, Emma noticed a soft, glowing light several feet away. The light moved from left to right, and then suddenly appeared in front of her. It was Kia, her translucent wings sending a faint glow that lit up the dark tunnel. She giggled and then darted away again.

"Your wings," Emma said. "They glow."

"The wings themselves do not," Kia said, looking over her shoulder at her wings. "The oil does." Kia noticed Emma's furrowed brow, and went on.

"Woven together are fairy wings," she said. "From a special fiber the tiniest of stiches are made." Emma was amazed. She would never have guessed that each wing was handmade, intricately woven into a masterpiece of artistry and design. It reminded her of the lone wing back at Grams' house. Had that wing been woven as well? Perhaps that is why it held up so well after all these years.

"Fairies a special oil use to coat the fiber. With this oil light does come," Kia said, hovering in front of Emma. Emma noticed that the wings seemed to pulse, giving off a consistent rhythm of light in the darkness. The faint glow reminded her of fireflies, their staccato messages filling the summer night sky.

"Emma," Kia said, leading the way. "Confusion is ahead. Do as I say you must."

"Ok," Emma said; again her brow furrowed.

"No, important it is," Kia insisted. "The Mimickers live here. Confusion they use as a weapon. You must my voice listen to."

"I get it, Kia," Emma said. "You want me to follow your directions."

"Yes," Kia said, not convinced that Emma fully understood. "To do so will help you leave. Alive."

"Alive?" Emma hung on the word.

"Some seekers have gone mad and do not leave," Kia answered. "You will see, when we enter." As Kia spoke, the tunnel grew lighter and lighter. Emma noticed a large opening off to the left. She slowly walked over and peered in.

"Oh my," she whispered, transfixed by what she saw.

≕⊦⊦≓

The fairy land is a pretty big place. The fairies take the boy to different spots so that he can see parts of the land. They walk through the forest (the boy knows what a forest looks like), they see a river (the boy knows what a river looks like), and they finally stop in this open area.

Let me describe the open area to you: it is open. And big. There aren't any trees—they are back in the forest. It's pretty rocky, and it stops suddenly—like there is a cliff. The boy walks to the edge and looks around. What he sees is pretty cool—a black swirling mass that disappears far below.

There are mountains everywhere. These aren't your typical Rocky Mountains, no sir. These mountains are big, and dark, and…scary.

No, not scary. I can't think of the right word…

--JPC

CHAPTER TWELVE

When Emma was little, her parents took her to a county carnival. It was her first experience with amusement park rides and clowns. However, nothing captured her attention more than the "Hall of Mirrors," a long, rectangular building that held different rooms. Each room was filled with different floor-to-ceiling mirrors. In one room, Emma discovered mirrors that distorted her shape, making her body small and her head large. She remembered giggling hysterically as her parents acted silly in front of the mirrors. Another room held mirrors that made all three Campbells very thin. Emma had stuck her tongue out, and had been surprised to find that even her tongue was a thin sliver of its real self. The largest room in the "Hall of Mirrors" again had floor-to-ceiling mirrors. However, these mirrors were at different angles, making it difficult to figure out what objects in the room were real and what objects were mere reflections. For a moment, young Emma had panicked in that room. Where were her parents? She could see their reflections, but when she reached out to touch her mother and father, she was only met with hard glass. It wasn't until she heard her parents' voices guiding her that the panic began to disappear.

The memory of that day rushed back as Emma stood at the entrance to a large cavern, taking in the scene before her. The cavern itself must have been over 100 feet in both height and width. At various points along the circumference were other entrances, all connected with stone bridges leading to the center of the cavern. Under the bridges a swirling water current churned, its sounds echoing in the chamber. Along the rocky walls were thousands of tiny mirrors—or what Emma first thought were mirrors. As she looked, she noticed that the mirrors were moving, silently flapping, and creating spontaneous spotlights around the room. The movement of light reminded her of a large disco ball.

In the middle of the cavern, a large object stood. Emma could only describe the object as a gigantic stalagmite, rising from the cavernous floor and disappearing through a large hole in the ceiling. Made of translucent glass, its surface was smooth and sheen.

Emma cautiously stepped onto the rock bridge leading to the center of the cavern. The suspended mirrors merged as partners, each side taking on the role of a single wing. She took another step. The mirrors moved closer.

Strange, Emma thought to herself.

"What are they?" she whispered to Kia who was hovering nearby. Other whispers immediately filled the cavern.

"What are they?"

"Are they?"

"What?"

"They are the Mimickers," Kia said. No sooner had the words left her mouth, then a frenzy started. The Mimickers spoke in voices identical to Kia's voice.

"They are the Mimickers!"

"We are the Mimickers!"

"We are!"

"We are not!"

"Mimickers, Mimickers, Mimickers!"

"We mimic!"

"Mimic, mimic!"

"We are not Mimickers!"

Emma stood still, wishing the chaos to stop. Just as it had started suddenly, it ended abruptly. She looked around. No movement. No noise. She inhaled and began walking slowly towards the middle.

As soon as she moved, the mirrors began to move. They linked with nearby mirrors, forming a flying V and, flapping loudly, converged on her, their swirling formation beginning at the highest point of the cavern and extending downward. They flew dangerously close to Emma, causing her to gasp and duck.

"What are you doing?" she yelled. The answers came in hundreds of voices identical to her own.

"What are you doing?"

"You are doing what?"

"What? What? What?"

"You!"

"Are you doing?"

"We are doing what?"

"Stop it!" Emma cried. The Mimickers answered.

"Stop it!"

"Stop, stop, stop!"

"You stop!"

"Don't you stop!"

"You stop it!"

"It, it, it!"

The pounding in Emma's head was growing louder and louder, resonating the echoes filling the cavern. The Mimickers had a way of drowning out all thought.

How am I even supposed to hear Kia's directions above this noise? Emma thought. I can't even hear my own thoughts. Emma secretly regretted all the times she had mimicked her middle school teachers, realizing now how incredibly annoying the behavior really was.

"Do as I say, Emma," Kia said. A thousand Kia voices responded.

"Do as I say!"

"No, as I say!"

"Don't do!"

"As I say!"

"Say, say, say!"

"Do say as I do!"

"Go to the center," Kia said. The mirrors replied.

"Don't go to the center!"

"Go to the center!"

"Go! Go! Go!"

"Center don't!"

Emma stood still. She was sure that Kia had said to move to the center of the cavern, but with the thousands of voices—all sounding like Kia's—doubt was starting to creep in. What if Kia had actually said not to move to the center of the cavern? What if she made a mistake? The mistake would be very costly if her life was on the line.

"Emma, move to the…" Kia didn't have a chance to finish her sentence. The mimickers took over.

"Don't move!"

"Emma, Emma, Emma!"

"Move to the...!"

"Move!"

"Where do I move to, Kia?" Emma asked. Thousands of Emmas broke out in song.

"I move!"

"Where?"

"Kia, Kia, Kia!"

"Where do I move?"

"Where, Kia?"

Emma didn't move or talk for some time. She let the calmness settle in the cavern once again. She stood still and began to think of everything she had observed about the Mimickers thus far.

The Mimickers had taken on the shape of mirrors, Emma thought to herself. That made sense, because they were mimicking whoever was standing in front of the mirrors. She looked around and saw partial images of herself reflected in hundreds of mirrors. It reminded her of pieces of a jigsaw puzzle. Yet, this jigsaw puzzle was moving and constantly changing, taking on a life of its own.

When I move, they move, she thought to herself. They mimic my motion. This was evident with the few steps she had taken, only to be dive-bombed by the flying mirrors. When she stopped moving, they stopped. Motion creates energy, she realized. Yet, she was careful to notice that the mimickers stayed clear of the central glass tower, which gave off its own source of energy.

Emma also noted that the Mimickers repeated words and phrases that she and Kia used in conversation, using matching tones so that it was extremely difficult to tell what Kia had said. Could she distinguish Kia's voice from the Mimickers? Emma didn't think so, and she wasn't willing to take the chance. After all, Kia had said to do as she says—this was the only way to leave the cavern alive.

If I can't tell what Kia is saying apart from what the Mimickers say, how am I supposed to follow Kia's instructions? Emma asked herself. She had to think of a way to separate Kia's voice from the Mimickers. But how? How could she communicate with Kia without the Mimickers interfering? How could she move to the center of the cavern without creating energy?

When the idea came, Emma felt foolish for not thinking of it sooner. Of course. It was the perfect solution for communicating with a fairy. Emma looked around and saw Kia. She made eye contact with Kia briefly, then closed her eyes and concentrated.

Kia, Emma thought, concentrating intently. *Kia, do you hear me?*

Silence. Then Kia answered.

You I hear, Emma. The words slowly dissolved into Emma's brain as though she were having a conversation under water. Emma didn't dare look at Kia for fear of setting off the Mimickers again, but a faint smile formed on her lips.

Ok, Kia. I am ready. Tell me what to do.

To the center of the cavern you must move. Slowly.

Emma took a few steps and then stopped. The mirrors jumped up and fluttered. Too fast. She stopped and waited, her heart rate slowing. She breathed in, held her breath, and then exhaled. She determined that the process of moving to the center of the cavern was more about control and less about timing.

She took one step and waited. Only a few of the mirrors twitched. Good. Another step followed. Barely any twitching. Still another step. Emma methodically followed this pattern, carefully waiting for any response from the Mimickers. It took some time to move from the rock bridge to the center of the cavern, but at last she was standing next to the giant stalagmite.

Now, climb you must. Kia's voice was soft, so soft that Emma thought she had heard wrong.

"What?" she said out loud, and realized her mistake. The mirrors instantly fluttered about, chirping out "What?" as they stayed toward the top of the cavern. After a few moments, they settled down again.

What, Kia?

Climb, Emma.

Climb what?

The structure in front of you climb.

Ummm...are we looking at the same thing? Because I see a giant icicle in front of me.

Climb.

It's smooth and there aren't any footholds...

Climb.

...or handholds.

Climb.

Kia? How? It doesn't make sense.

Reach up, Emma.

But there's nothing there!

Go against your own belief.

I don't understand...

Climb.

Kia?

Trust me, Emma.

Emma stared at the glass structure. She ran her hand over the smooth surface. There was nothing to hold onto, nothing jutting out that she could use as a ledge. She shook her head, not able to comprehend how she was going to get to the top.

Reach out against all belief.

Belief tells me that this isn't logical, Emma thought. Belief tells me that this can't be done. Yet...

Trust me, Emma.

Emma blinked and, lifting her chin in a determined look, placed her foot against the glass structure. In the place where her foot touched the side, the glass began to glow and morph. To her surprise, a foothold formed underneath the sole of her shoe. With her opposite hand, she reached up, forming her fingers into a climbing grasp. Again, the structure glowed and changed, providing a handhold to support her.

Reach out against all belief.

Against all belief...

Believe...

The process was slow. Emma's hands ached, red marks embedded in her skin evidence of the physical strain. Her legs shook from nervousness or exhaustion. Or both. Little by little she ascended the glass tower, Kia hovering closely the entire time. Numerous times Emma had to stop and wipe sweat from her brow, or reposition her hands and feet. When she was near the top, Emma looked down one last time. The Mimickers were slowly fluttering in their places, waiting for motion, words—anything–to enter their world again and give them life.

Well, that won't be me, Emma thought to herself. I am done with this place. With that, she disappeared into the hole above, Kia lighting the way.

I just read what I already wrote down. It sounds stupid, I know. I am not even into fairies or flowers or stuff like that. I am only writing down this dream that I keep having. Maybe if I write it down it will stop bothering me...

I don't understand how the boy can be so trusting. Personally, I would freak out if I came face-to-face with a fairy. He doesn't. Maybe it's because he is a boy who just believes things...

--JPC

CHAPTER THIRTEEN

"Trust." The word was said so softly, Emma wasn't sure that Kia had heard her. She waited and watched Kia working quietly in a small, secluded cave inside the mountain. After the mental and physical struggle of the mimickers, Emma welcomed rest. She tried to stoke the conversation again.

"I figured out what I needed to gain from the cave and the Mimickers," Emma said. "It's trust."

Kia stopped what she was doing and looked at Emma.

"Correct you are," Kia said. "To have trust, you must believe. In someone. Whom do you believe in?"

Emma hadn't thought that far into the discovery. Trust involves two people, or perspectives of a situation. Trust is needed in the face of fear, when everything might look bleak and hopeless. Who did Emma trust? A year ago, the answer would have been obvious. Dad. He had always been there for her, helping her, giving her advice—but now he was gone. Did she feel that same way about her mom? Emma sadly realized that she didn't—at least, not yet. Mom was Mom, there to pick up the pieces, organize things, and make sure that Emma was taken care of. She didn't feel the same connection to Mom that she had to Dad. Perhaps that's why it was so hard.

"I...I don't know," Emma said. "In the cavern, I couldn't see a way out. The Mimickers were constantly talking, and it was so confusing. And then you told me to climb that ridiculous glass tower..."

"And you did," Kia said. "Why?"

Emma thought for a moment. Why did she follow Kia's directions? After all, Kia hadn't been entirely welcoming to her at the beginning, and there was no love lost between the two.

Yet, things had changed. Kia had saved her from certain death in the abyss by bending time, a task that exhausted even the well-trained fairy. Kia knew the land well, and she was given instructions specifically by Del. Emma didn't feel in danger when she was with Kia; in fact, she felt safe when the fairy was close by.

"I climbed the tower," Emma said, "because I trusted you."

Kia smiled. "A start, it is. Flattered am I that you trust me, but there is more. Whom else do you trust?"

Emma thought some more. It was easy to say that she trusted Kia—now. Kia had proven her trust as well. Who else was there to trust?

Me. Her brain slowly formed around the word hidden deep inside her.

Trusting Kia was one thing—Kia knew everything about the land and the people. Trusting herself brought Emma to a whole new level. Trusting herself to believe that she could figure out a way to communicate with Kia where the Mimickers wouldn't interfere. Trusting herself to climb a glass tower without handholds or footholds. Trusting herself to be the one that could save £areä, the fairies, Grams, and ultimately herself. The progression from courage to trust was not lost on Emma.

"Good it is to trust others," Kia said. "But if you do not trust yourself, all is lost. You must trust yourself when the shape-shifters you meet. Your own intuition you must use to defeat them."

Emma thought about what Kia said. While she was still nervous about the final meeting with the shape-shifters, something had changed. *She* had changed. No longer did the words "fearful" and "scared" play in the forefront of her mind. She was developing other traits, other characteristics that were needed. Yet something about this formed a question in her mind.

"Kia," Emma said. "Why do I have to be the one to save £areä? I mean, you obviously have courage, and you trust your instincts. Why can't it be you?"

Kia looked away for a brief moment, and then turned her attention back to Emma. "*Find the three, and the fourth will find you.*"

"The prophecy," Emma confirmed, but shook her head. "I don't understand."

"Fairies are not capable of finding the three," Kia said. "Abilities we have, and they are well. But finding the three we cannot do. If we cannot find the three, the fourth will not be made known to us, and we do not have the power to overcome the shape-shifters."

So I am the only one who can find the three, Emma thought to herself. Courage, trust, and...

She wondered what the third lesson would be, and how this would help the fourth to be revealed. What would the fourth be? Would it be revealed to her in time? Would Emma have enough time to save the fairies and Grams?

Kia interrupted her thoughts.

"Emma," Kia said. "What is it like—to have a family?"

"What do you mean? Don't you have a family?" Emma asked, surprised.

Kia shook her head. "The other fairies I am closest to, but a family I do not have."

Emma was speechless. She had just assumed that Kia had parents and brothers and sisters living somewhere in the Castle of the Trees. To know that Kia was alone explained her tough attitude and willingness to go on the quest—both being evidence of protecting herself from loneliness.

"Well," Emma said slowly, "it's ok. I mean, it's nice. You have people you can count on, who will always take care of you and never leave you." As soon as the words were spoken, Emma winced. Well, at least that's what is supposed to happen.

"Close you are to these people?" Kia asked.

Emma thought for a moment. A day ago, she would have questioned her response, but since she had arrived in £areä and learned about her family connection, she wanted to say yes.

"I think that I am learning how to be closer," she said.

Kia smiled. "That I wish for as well."

Silence hung in the air as the two processed through their thoughts. Emma wanted to ask more questions, but waited until Kia talked.

"Parents I had, yes," Kia said. "Know them I do not. In the forest I was found as a fairy babe by surveyors, inhabitants of £areä that scout the land. They took me to the High Councilor—your Del— who raised me in the Castle of the Trees."

"And you don't know how or why you were alone in the forest?" Emma asked. Kia shook her head.

"My story no one knows, only when I arrived. The High Councilor gifted me a special skill," Kia continued. "That is why I know how to bend time." She paused for a moment, and then went on. "The other fairies, they are my family. Yet, the same it is not. Days there are that I wish for what I do not have. My own family."

A sudden thought came to Emma.

"Kia," Emma said. "Have you ever gone outside of £areä? Like, to explore?"

Kia shook her head. "Just to save you was I in the woods."

"Do you ever want to go back in the woods?" Emma asked.

Kia was quiet for a moment.

"Sometimes…" she said softly. "Wonder do I that there might be more—more to see, more to discover…" Though the words stopped, the thought of more lingered in the air for some time. Emma couldn't help but notice that both Kia and Grams had a distinct drive to discover, that both longed for more than just what £areä, as beautiful as it was, had to offer. Yet Grams chose to leave. Where did that leave Kia?

The conversation ended as the two settled into a comfortable silence. Emma's last thoughts before sleep overtook her were of what might lay ahead for both Kia and her.

The whole time the boy is gone, he isn't alone. Well, he is the only boy in the fairy land, but he isn't alone. The fairies are with him. Sometimes they are next to him. Sometimes they are in the trees, watching him.

The time he likes the most is when he talks with them.

It sounds just like wind chimes…

--JPC

CHAPTER FOURTEEN

Emma stopped to catch her breath. She had been walking for hours through various caves deep inside the mountain range, so long that she had lost all sense of direction. The strenuous work was difficult and exhausting. The tunnels connecting the caverns were not well lit and, while she was thankful for Kia's lighted wings, it was still hard to see what little path there was. Oftentimes she found herself stumbling.

The caves themselves were beautiful. As a young girl, Emma had been to Meramec Caverns in southern Missouri while staying with relatives. She had traveled along the walkways, observing the gigantic stalagmites and stalactites. She remembered the cool crispness of the caverns, along with the absolute darkness when all of the flashlights were turned off. The sudden panic of being in a room and not being able to see anything had forced her to cry out. Only the comfort of her father's hand had calmed her.

The memories of that trip were similar to what she was seeing now, except for the light. Wherever Emma looked, the rock formations glowed a dim light. Their light moved and emitted different colors—red, pink, yellow, blue, green. The glowing lights radiated warmth, sereneness, and contentedness—filling the caverns with colors of the rainbow. The lights slowly pulsed, faded, and then grew brighter, and then faded again as though they were performing a visual symphony. There was a chill in the air, but Emma wasn't cold. In fact, the glowing lights stirred a warm spirit inside of her, an anticipation of what was to come.

Perhaps the excitement of the atmosphere was attributed to Emma's knowledge that the journey was reaching its end. They were approaching the third lesson, the final item that would help her defeat the shape-shifters, and save £areä, and also Grams. She had received courage and trust, two important traits. Now that she had both, she realized how absent they had been in her life before £areä. How different life was now! How different *she* was now.

Emma was so focused on her own thoughts that she missed a step, tumbling onto the hard, rocky surface of the cave. She braced the fall with her hands, only to feel a jolt of pain.

"Ouch!" Emma sat on the ground rubbing her sore wrist.

"Hurt, you are?" Kia asked.

"Just a fall," Emma replied, shaking out her hand. "I'll be ok."

Kia hovered in place until Emma stood up.

"Here I must go," Kia said.

"Go? Emma asked, confused. "What do you mean?"

"To leave you I must," Kia said quietly.

"Wait! You can't leave," Emma cried. "We're almost to the end, and besides, how will I know what to do? Where to go? You are my guide."

"Leave, I must," Kia said, a hint of sadness in her voice. "Remember—the three I cannot find." Emma then realized that staying was not in Kia's ability. While she wanted to stay, she could not be in the presence of the third lesson. Why?

"Some lessons fairies have, Emma," Kia answered. "No fairy has all. This lesson I cannot have. Leave I must."

"Del said you have to lead me to the destination," Emma argued. "Where do I go? How will I know when I am there?"

"Through that portal you must go," Kia pointed toward an opening. It was unlike any other cave opening they had entered. This entrance was a single stone doorway that curved in a half-circle on top. On either side of the entrance were ornate columns, silently announcing that something different was on the other side.

Through the entrance faint light filtered through. Emma could make out shapes of trees—evergreens mostly—that filled the doorway frame. Trillium dotted the forest landscape, standing still. A narrow dirt path led from the entrance into the forest. The scene look oddly familiar.

You will know.

Emma looked back into the cave, but it was too late. Kia was gone.

You will know.
You will know.

How will I know? Emma thought to herself as she ventured through the doorway into the forest. She slowly walked on the path, looking around her. The ground was covered in new vegetation, flowers just beginning to open, grass standing tall in its early stage of life. She glanced back at the open doorway—but it wasn't there. The entrance was gone. She was all alone, and the only way forward was through the forest.

Emma walked for some time on the dirt path, ducking under low-lying branches and stepping around large, exposed roots. She didn't know where the path led, but the calmness she felt confirmed that this was the way she was supposed to go. The forest was so real—the smells, the touch, the feel. Yet there was something missing. Emma stopped and listened for something—anything—that she could connect with, that would give her clues about her current surroundings. But it wasn't there. In fact, nothing was there.

Sound.

There was no sound. No birds chirping, no rustle of the wind, no trees swaying.

Just stillness.

It was like watching a silent movie and imagining what the actors were saying.

Except there aren't any other actors here, Emma thought. Just me.

A small seed of anxiety began to stir inside of her, but she quickly set it aside to focus on the task at hand. The steady beating of her heart filled in the silence.

The forest itself was familiar—too familiar. Turns in the path exposed memories, which sparked a sense of personal connection deep inside Emma.

I've been here before, she thought to herself. The trees, the forest, the path, the clearing ahead...

The forest by Grams' house.

Emma looked around for a glimpse of Grams' house, but there was none. Yet, she knew with every fiber in her being that this forest was somehow linked to Grams' house, that the familiarity was not a coincidence. She was meant to be here.

She slowly walked into the clearing, the clearing that looked exactly like the one she had been in a day before when the shape-shifters had come. There was no sign of the shape-shifters now, only trees and the splintered light that slipped past the branches, exposing narrow openings in the forest darkness. And silence. Always the lingering stillness.

What lesson am I supposed to learn? She stood still, looking around her. She was supposed to be here, waiting. Waiting for what?

Then it happened. The crack of a twig broke the stillness like a gunshot. Emma spun around and gasped. In front of her stood a young boy, perhaps six or seven years old. In his hand he carried a worn baseball glove.

"Who are you?" he asked.

≍⊰⊱≍

The boy is gone for a long time. Well, I should explain that it feels like a long time, but it is in fairy time. It doesn't match up with real world time. (Does that make sense? If it doesn't, oh well. I'm just telling a story here.)

So, the boy gets a little nervous. I think he is worried that his mom is going to find out and he will be in big trouble, so the fairies send him on his way. Not completely—they keep an eye on him because they are flying high up in the trees. He is walking through the forest, and that's when something strange happens.

He meets a girl.

--JPC

CHAPTER FIFTEEN

"Who are you?" the boy asked again, tilting his head as he looked at her.

"I'm…I'm Emma," Emma blurted out, staring at the boy. His fair complexion was framed by flaxen-colored hair. His blue eyes looked at her quizzically as he tried to locate some sense of logic in his young mind.

"Oh," the boy said, kicking at the dirt. "I'm James." Emma's heart skipped at the mention of his name, her eyes still on the baseball mitt firmly in the boy's grip. Her mind raced, trying to connect the information and make some sense of it. How could it be? How could it be that she was standing in front of her dad—and yet, he wasn't her dad? He was just a boy.

Time overlaps and intertwines...

She slowly shook her head, trying to create reason, but her efforts were futile.

Even though she was sure she knew the answer, an invisible force pushed her to ask the question. "Why are you in the forest, James?"

The boy looked at her, a guilty look covering his face. "My baseball went into the forest. I know that Mom said to never go through the gate, but I had to find my baseball. It was my lucky baseball." He looked up at Emma suddenly. "Have you seen it?"

Emma shook her head.

"Oh, well," the boy said. "At least I had fun here. I made some new friends."

"The fairies?" Emma asked. The boy's eyes lit up with excitement.

"Yes! Do you know the fairies, too?" he said.

Emma nodded. "I do. They're pretty neat, right? Although, I am thinking that they should be our little secret, don't you think?" The boy nodded.

"My mom won't believe me if I tell her about fairies," he said. Emma smiled. She was pretty sure that if her dad told Grams about the fairies, Grams *would* understand.

"It's ok. My mom wouldn't understand if I told her about fairies either." Emma studied the boy. There were parts of him that were new to her, but other parts that were so, so familiar. The way he smiled—he had that same smile the last time she saw him. And the twinkle in his eye, announcing that mischief was around the corner. Oh, how she missed that! It was almost too much for her. Emma bit her lip to keep from crying out.

"Why are you in the forest?" James asked.

Emma thought for a moment. How do you explain to a six-year-old that you are on a quest to search for unknown traits in order to fight an evil so dangerous, it could destroy your entire family? She was sure it would be enough to scare him off completely. Then again, it was almost enough to scare her off as well.

"I guess you could say that I am looking for something, too," Emma said.

"Is it a baseball?" James asked. Emma laughed.

"No, it isn't a baseball. It's something…different."

"Can I help?" James said.

Emma's heart silently tore at the plea of the young child. She was conflicted—she knew that she had to find the last gift, the last lesson. Grams needed her, and time was important. In order to save £areä, she had to destroy the crown. Every minute put Grams and the fairies in more danger. Yet, she also knew with every ounce of her being that she was supposed to be here—in this moment—talking to the young boy.

Her father.

Emma smiled. "Sure, but while we look, maybe we could talk…and hang out together, ok?"

"Like friends?" he said.

"Like friends," Emma nodded. She hopped off the log and motioned for James to follow.

"I don't have any friends," James said as they walked in the forest. Emma looked at the boy as he kicked at the dirt path again.

"Why is that?" she asked.

"Well," James began, "we don't live by anybody. And my mom doesn't let me go over to other houses to play."

How lonely, Emma thought. To be by yourself all the time and not have friends to play with. She wondered why Grams hadn't allowed her father to form friendships with other boys. Was Grams afraid of what others would think? Was she worried that others would notice something different about the family, or that maybe too many questions would be asked and answers would be harder and harder to form? Was it too difficult to hide the past? Did Grams still think of the past? She hadn't realized the loneliness her father had felt as a child. He had never talked about it. How could she have known?

"Except now I have you," James said, smiling. "You're my first friend." He laughed and sprinted ahead of Emma, jumping over a fallen log and hiding behind a large tree trunk.

"Hmmm…" Emma teased, "you think you're so fast, do you?" She took off after the young boy, his squeals of delight filling the forest air. They ran and ran, tagging each other, teasing each other like old friends playing on a sunny summer afternoon.

When their muscles ached and the game grew old, they stood by the edge of the tranquil water pool and skipped stones across the water. James, as young as he was, was an expert stone thrower. He showed Emma how to skip the same stone four times across the surface of the water. Her own efforts did not prove as successful as the young boy's achievements.

Emma finally sat down on a large rock jutting out into the open pool. She dipped her bare feet in the cool water and sighed. James stood a few feet away on the bank, trolling a stick underneath the surface. She looked at him—her father, the boy mingled together—and the intertwining feelings began to well up inside of her. His crooked smile. His messed-up hair. His laugh. A tear slowly fell down her cheek as her emotions rose.

A perfect day. A perfect day that would come to an end.

"Are you sad?" James asked, standing still.

"Why do you ask that?" Emma said, inconspicuously wiping the tear away.

"You look sad," James said. "My mom looks like that when she is sad."

"No, not sad," she said. "Perhaps a little, but more happy than anything. It's been a long time since I've been happy. A really long time."

"Why?" James asked. "There's lots of things to be happy about." Emma chuckled. Even though the person standing next to her was just a boy, his words sounded so much like the 40-something version she grew to love.

"Someone I loved very much," Emma said, "had to leave."

"He left?" James said. "That's not very nice."

"He couldn't help it," Emma explained. "I think that if he had the choice, he would have stayed, but he couldn't…"

"You mean, like he died?" James whispered. Emma nodded, realizing that the boy was smarter than she gave him credit for.

"Yes, he died," Emma said, the words causing pain deep inside of her. "It's been hard to go on without him."

The boy thought for a moment. "He must have been very important to you."

"He was," Emma replied.

"My mom always says that memories help us to remember people. Maybe they can help you." James looked up at Emma and smiled.

"You might be right," Emma said.

"Do you have good memories?" the boy asked.

"The best memories," Emma said, looking out at the water, and she meant it. They sat together next to the water's edge for some time—boy, girl, father, daughter, friends—not talking, just being together. Finally, James stood up.

"I should go," he said. "My mom is probably worried about me."

Emma nodded. She could easily see Grams frantically searching for James if she already realized he was missing. She stood up and joined him.

"It's been fun playing with you," James said.

"Likewise," Emma smiled and waved as he started jogging down the forest path. She turned and began to head back to the clearing.

"Wait, Emma," a voice said. It was James. He had come back. Before she could respond, his arms were wrapped around her waist, his head pressed firmly against her.

"Thank you for today," James said, looking up at her, a smile stretched wide across his face. At that moment, a sense of peace covered Emma.

"Thank you, James," she replied, and she meant it. Instantly, a flash of bright light engulfed them both, blinding them. A force so powerful ripped Emma away, and she felt herself thrown against the forest ground. She lay motionless for some time, trying to catch her breath. Her eyes were closed, but she could feel and smell the dampness, a wetness all around her. Rain was falling as the sky hung low.

When she finally was able to breathe again, Emma opened her eyes. Even before she looked around, she knew that James was gone. Through the dim light, she could make out the outlines of trees. The forest. She was still in the forest clearing.

She sat up and looked around. This was the forest—but it was Gram's forest. She was sure of it. She tried to catch a glimpse of the path, but it wasn't there. Although the cold, wetness of the forest caused the air to chill, the cool temperature was not the catalyst that sent shivers suddenly coursing through her body. The cause for the trembling was the sudden realization that she wasn't alone.

The shape-shifters were waiting.

The boy meets the girl, and they talk. I don't know what they talk about. That part is a bit fuzzy for me, but it's like they are friends or something. After that, the boy says goodbye…

And that's where the dream ends.

I know what you're thinking—what?? How can the dream end there? Remember, it is a dream. It doesn't have to make sense. I am just writing this down so I have something to turn in.

But I wish I knew what happened after the boy said goodbye…

Maybe someday the dream will be finished.

--JPC

CHAPTER SIXTEEN

When Emma was young, her parents took her to meet her maternal great-grandmother, Henrietta Barker. Mrs. Barker lived in the Sunny Blossom Nursing Home, a facility committed to caring for the aged and elderly.

For Emma, the trip to the nursing home was unlike any other experience. Her innocent shyness was completely lost on well-intentioned residents who tried to grab her hands, pat her face, or even pull her struggling body onto their wheelchairs for a ride. To them, young Emma was a new visitor, someone that would help them connect to the outside world. For her, however, they were strangers, and she did the one thing that she was taught to do when she came into contact with strangers. She screamed.

Not until Emma arrived in great-grandma Barker's room did she finally calm down. While James and Trudy made small talk with great-grandma, Emma walked around the room, looking at the different objects. There were the usual things one would find in a nursing home—the walker, the multi-colored afghan, the memorable trinkets. On a wooden table next to the century-old dresser sat an oval mirror. On top of the mirror sat a collection of bottles, all brightly colored and filled with various liquids.

"Bring one here, child," great-grandma Barker called out softly. Emma obeyed and picked up the nearest bottle. It was amber colored, with a funny looking balloon on the top. Great-grandma held the bottle in her left hand, and turning over Emma's wrist, carefully squeezed the balloon, sending a fine mist out the end of the long tube.

"Well, what does it smell like?" great-grandma Barker asked. Emma lifted her wrist and smelled. She closed her eyes and tried to think hard.

"The sun," she said, opening her eyes. Great-grandma Barker smiled and nodded. Years later, even after great-grandma Barker had passed away and the items in the nursing home room had been packed up and donated to various places, thoughts brought Emma back to that day. She often caught a glimpse of the amber-colored bottle sitting on her own dresser, and every so often she would spray a fine mist in the air and smile. Scent had a way of bringing back memories.

That is why, when Emma found herself in the woods, dampness all around her, she knew she wasn't alone. Even before she saw them, she knew the shape-shifters were near. She could smell the foul, acrid mist that lingered in the air, moving closer and closer. That distinct smell of danger, of death, that brought back such horrid memories was close. Its scent permeated her nostrils, causing bile to rise up from her throat. Emma fought the panic by breathing slowly and evenly. As she sat up, she noticed the shadows beginning to form around the inner edges of the clearing.

Patience, Del had said. *Patience. Kill you they will not. You they need. You are the key to their plan. They feed off your fear. Patience, Emma.*

Emma repeated Del's words over and over in her head, her fingers subconsciously touching the crown deep in her pocket. She watched as the grey mist grew closer and closer. It broke off and branched out to either side of the clearing, soon surrounding her. She barely moved, only watching its actions out of the corner of her vision. The rings of grey began forming evil images in front of her—hands with sharp nails, wolves with bared teeth, large eyes watching down on her. Emma's heartrate jumped.

She who steps into the unknown.
She who steps into the unknown.
Breathe.
Slowly.
Have courage.

As an image of a hollow skull charged her, Emma suddenly stood up and closed her eyes. She felt the mist brush against her face, but the image itself vanished. Slowly pleasant scenes from the Castle of the Trees filled her mind, calming her.

Have courage.

But I'm scared, Emma thought to herself. Suddenly, Kia's words spoke to her.

Emma, courage appears in the midst of fear, Kia had said. *Courage defeats fear.*

The shape-shifters became frustrated and hissed, whispering messages into her brain.

"Surrender…"
"You will fail…"
"You are nothing…"
"You are nothing!"
"Nothing…"
"Nothing…"
"Nothing!"

Something broke inside of Emma at that moment. She was tired of being afraid. She was tired of being sad. She was tired of feeling out of control, of not having choices in life. Most of all, she was tired of being alone. She opened her eyes and stared at the mist.

Reach out against all belief.

Trust.

Believe.

In Yourself.

"You're wrong," Emma said. "I am something." She dug into her pocket and pulled the crown out, holding it in her outstretched palm. "You want this so bad? Come and get it." She closed her fingers around the crown and clutched it to her chest, waiting for the shape-shifters to come.

And they did.

The dark gray mist swirled around her, pulling at her, pushing her. In the midst of the wind force, she struggled to keep standing. It felt as if the shadows were pulling her apart. The shape-shifters screamed terrifying cries as they formed a cyclone, swallowing her. Instantly, the earth opened up and she fell down, down, freefalling far below to the unknown, the swirling vortex holding her tight in its grasp.

Emma landed with a heavy thud on a flat surface, the sudden jolt of the contact causing her to cry out. She could still smell the wretched mist, so she knew the shape-shifters were close by. After she checked her limbs to make sure that there were no broken bones, she slowly sat up and surveyed her surroundings.

A thin stream of light from high above helped Emma see where she was. Indeed, she had landed on a hard surface. It was comparable to concrete and its round shape was barely large enough for her to lay across. Emma tried to stand up, but instantly realized that something was wrong. When she shifted her weight to her right foot to stand, the surface began to tilt down. When she stepped back, the surface righted itself again. She inched her foot toward the edge, and the surface slowly descended.

It's weight-bearing, Emma thought. She would need to be very careful so as not to fall off. She lowered herself down again and lay flat on her stomach. Inching her way to the edge, she stopped every couple of moments to make sure the surface was balanced. When she felt comfortable, she looked over the edge, and gasped at what she saw.

Below her was a large, swirling whirlpool, the waters churning clockwise. The outer rings of water held tiny flames of fire, but as Emma's eyes moved toward the center, the flames gathered more and more, spinning at a faster speed than the water itself. The inner currents created a centrifugal force within the center of the pool, allowing the flames to form a fiery tornado that crept upward. Although the pool of water and fire was far below, Emma could hear the rush of the force and feel the heat as it reached up to touch her.

How odd that both water and fire exist in the same pool, Emma thought. Opposites moving together. She turned her attention to the rest of the scene below.

A large, circular corridor extended along the circumference of the pool. At first, the lack of adequate light prevented Emma from seeing the shadows moving in and out of the corridor. When her vision focused, her eyes grew wide. Far below were snakes—gigantic snakes writhing in and out, over and under one another, their hisses echoing throughout the chamber. She watched as they turned on each other, baring large fangs, and then dismissed the threat, only to challenge the next contender.

Emma's stomach turned. It had to be snakes, of course. Of all the things she was afraid of, snakes were at the top of the list. Ever since her encounter with a snake at summer camp last year, Emma hadn't been particularly fond of the reptile. It didn't matter that it was a harmless garter snake; the back and forth motion of the slithering animal was enough to make Emma ant to turn and run.

The shape-shifters would know that, Emma realized. After all, they can smell fear. Even Del had said that they feed on fear. They know what I am afraid of. The thought of this began to stir anxiety deep inside her. She quickly shook her head to refocus her attention to the task at hand—finishing her observations.

The last part of observing her environment proved to be the most challenging for Emma. It involved carefully looking under the circular surface itself. Carefully was an understatement; Emma had to gingerly move inch by inch in order to achieve this goal, all the while checking and rechecking the balance of the surface. Her heart raced anytime the surface began to move, fearful that it wouldn't stop but instead tilt to the point that she would slide off. When she finally did achieve an accurate viewpoint of what the surface was indeed balancing on, she blinked.

There was nothing there.

The round, concrete surface was suspended in air. Just air.

How am I supposed to get off this thing? Emma thought. There was nothing to jump to, climb on, or reach out and grab hold of. She was trapped on a floating surface, high above the churning water and fire below as snakes slithered about. Not the most ideal situation to be in. Emma made her way back to the middle of the surface and sat upright, hugging her knees.

Find the three, and the fourth will find you.

The three.

It was clearly evident that courage was the first gift Emma received, and now she understood why. Courage was an essential part of the strategy to defeat the shape-shifters. She knew its importance and she acknowledged its absence before the journey. She was silently thankful that Del knew that as well and had insisted on the quest to prepare her.

So, I have courage, Emma noted. The shape-shifters feed on fear, and courage defeats fear. I can use it to my advantage. What else do I have?

Trust. Her thoughts brought her back to the cave of the Mimickers, and how her trust in Kia and in herself had guided her. What would have happened had she not been able to trust Kia, or had doubted her own intuitiveness? Emma shuddered at the thought. However, she would have to rely on her own thoughts to make it through the final challenge.

What is the third gift, then? Emma sat perplexed as she sorted out her thoughts. She was sure it had something to do with meeting the boy—her father—in the forest. To be honest, though, she had been lost in the experience too much to focus on the lesson that she had to learn. She had so much wanted to soak in every minute—no, every second—with her father that she forgot the past, or the future. She simply lived in the present, content with just being a teenage girl spending time with a young boy, laughing and crying, emotions intertwined in just being. It was enough, and it was good. So good.

That which accepts what has been given as good.

Been given as good.

Accept.

As good.

Suddenly, Emma knew what the third gift was. A strangled cry escaped her throat.

Gratitude.

How strange it felt, like a foreign object deep inside her heart. It had been so long since she felt gratitude, she didn't know what to do or how to react. Her own grief had swallowed all other emotions, only allowing sadness and insecurity to show themselves. Was it alright to be thankful? Was she betraying her father by feeling contentedness? What if she forgot him? Emma shook her head.

"He isn't coming back," she whispered to herself. The words hung in the air, and then dissipated. Slowly, images filled her mind: a young boy in the forest, her father teaching her to ride her first bike, reading stories to her at bedtime. She felt his big arms around her, holding her in an embrace. She smelled his musky cologne lingering in the air.

Emma carefully stood up. She came to realize that forgetting wasn't an option. Her father had been right. Good memories were precious gifts.

I can't change what has happened, she thought. Oh, how I wish I could! But I can't.

But I am thankful.

So thankful…

He was my dad.

The tears falling down her cheeks were no longer the tears of sadness or sorrow. Instead, they were tears of laughter, tears of hope.

Tears of joy.

How different she felt, like a weight had been lifted off her shoulders. She wiped her eyes and looked around. She had changed—no, been changed—by the experiences within the last days. The events up to now were not lost on Emma. She still had a job to do. She must destroy the crown.

Del had been explicit in his instructions on how to go about the task of destroying the crown. There was only one way known to the fairies to destroy the crown and keep it from getting into the hands of the shape-shifters. The crown had to be thrown into the churning pool of water and fire.

Emma carefully looked over the edge at the violent waters below. The currents bellowed, calling to her. She reached into her pocket and retrieved the small crown.

"You're so small," she said, "and yet you caused so much trouble for a lot of people. No more, no more." With one swift motion, she launched the crown over the side of the levitating surface. Attracted by her sudden movements, the snakes rose up and watched as the crown disappeared into the waters below and screams filled the chambers.

Emma was just about to turn around when something moved near her. She tried to focus, but was suddenly hit in the face. As her hand came up to feel the trickle of blood caused by the cut on her cheek, she heard the clink-clink of something landing on the surface. She bent down to look closer.

When she saw it, she gasped.

The crown had come back.

CHAPTER SEVENTEEN

It wasn't supposed to happen this way.

Del had explained that the crown had to be thrown into the pool of water and fire. Emma did just that, but the crown had come back. Why?

"What have I done wrong?" Emma said out loud. "What did I forget?" It seemed so long ago when she had met with Del and he had given the instructions. Was there something she had missed? She replayed the quest in her mind.

Find the three...

A creature like no other, who steps into the unknown.

Who reaches against all belief.

That which accepts what has been given as good.

...and the fourth will find you.

Emma realized her mistake. The fourth was still missing.

"Well, this is a great time to be waiting for something," Emma sighed. "I am on top of a tilting platform, high above a water and fire tornado, surrounded by gigantic snakes. And I have to wait?" She listened to her own words, and then laughed. How would she ever explain to her classmates what she did over the weekend? She wouldn't. She couldn't even find the words to describe her journey, and she was pretty sure that even if she could, no one would believe her. In fact, Emma wasn't sure she believed it herself.

Emma carefully sat down in the middle of the surface. Her thoughts went over everything that had happened over the past few days, beginning at the arrival at Grams' house. It was true—she hadn't been excited about spending the weekend. Grams didn't seem to understand her, and she certainly didn't understand Grams. Different interests kept them apart. Of course, Emma now understood the reason why.

Entering the fairy world of £areä had been both surreal and exciting. At first, Emma had been scared. No doubt about it—fluttering fairies were an abstract thought in her mind. That is, until she met Del. He was kind and gentle. He exhibited patience that anyone could learn from. Emma realized that there was an unspoken connection with Del that she now missed. How she wished he was here with her! He would know what to do.

Strong you are, Del had said. *The three you will have. The fourth you must discover.*

Yes, the fourth.

Find the three, and the fourth will find you.
But what was the fourth?

Emma's mind continued to travel to recent memories. Seeing the beauty of the Castle of the Trees brought a smile to her face. The fairies had been so welcoming, taking her, a stranger, into their community. Did they know that she was the chosen one? Did they realize that she was their only hope? Emma shook her head, assured that their actions had been genuine and real, their hospitality wrapped in truth. The festival, the lights, the flowers—her mind couldn't accurately portray all the things she had experienced. Memories didn't do the setting justice.

No wonder Dad and Grams forgot, Emma thought to herself. It's too hard to even imagine that a place so beautiful exists. She secretly hoped that she would be able to hold on to the memories.

Her thoughts turned to Kia. Oh, Kia. How she had been mistaken about the pint-sized wonder! Yes, Kia was blunt, and fierce, and stubborn—but she was much more. Emma thought about how Kia took charge on the bridge. She remembered how Kia stayed calm in the cave of the Mimickers, and how sadness covered Kia's face when she said goodbye. Had she wanted to stay, or to leave? Was she sad because Emma was experiencing something she could not? Most importantly, where was Kia now?

Emma looked down at the crown resting on her open palm.

"All of this," Emma said, "because I touched the crown." She was about to accept this thought, when she suddenly stopped.

"No," Emma said. "It wasn't because I touched the crown, or because Dad chased a baseball. It started…it started with Grams." She stood up, sending the platform into a slight tilt. She quickly righted herself and continued her thought process.

"This whole thing started with Grams going into the forest—the Forbidden Zone," Emma said out loud. "It started with her choosing to leave £areä and live in my world." Emma knew why Grams had done it—Del had made that clear. Love was the foundation of the choice. Yet, what did the choice really mean? Sure, Grams had left her home of £areä, but she unconsciously lost so much more. Del had explained that she would never be able to come back. Communication had stopped; she had no ties back to her family, her people, or her land.

She had given up all. For love.

Suddenly, Emma realized what the fourth gift was.

Who gives all for all given.

Grams had given all for a new life in a new world. She had risked all to have the chance to experience love. And now, all was in danger. Yet Emma was the only one who could protect that life—no, save that life. How could Emma possibly save the fairies, Grams, and herself? She knew that the only way for the crown to be destroyed was for it to disappear in the churning waters below. She looked over the side of the surface again and shuddered. Hot smoke curled upward from the rising inferno of water and fire bellowing below. Steaming bubbles crashed against the sides of the pool.

Who gives all for all given.

Courage.

Trust.

Gratitude…

Grams had given all for one thing.

Love.

Who gives all for all given.

Love.

Love hopes all things.

Love believes all things.

Love does not delight in evil, but rejoices in truth.

Love is patient.

Love is kind…

The greatest of these is love.

Emma exhaled. She knew what the fourth gift was. She stood up and looked at the crown in her open hand. She curled her fingers tightly around the crown, and did the one thing she could do.

In love.

She jumped.

CHAPTER EIGHTEEN

All reason left Emma the moment her feet passed the edge of the platform. With the crown tucked firmly in her grasp, she opened her arms to the unknown below.

As she fell, she could see the fierce flames reaching up for her. She could feel the intense heat and hear the crackling coming from the hot roars of the fire below. Yet she couldn't figure out why the fire didn't touch her. She couldn't comprehend why the scorching flames didn't burn her skin or consume her completely.

As she continued down, the screams of the snakes filled her mind. She felt the rush of the mist as they charged, their force blowing at her full strength. Yet, she couldn't wrap her thoughts around why they didn't attack and devour her. She closed her eyes to block out the sight.

She could feel the wetness of the water as it violently churned around her, pulling at her, pushing her. She wasn't in the water itself; she could still breathe on her own, that fact was sure. Yet, she couldn't understand how the water had such control over her. She struggled against the chaotic currents, but they pulled her down, down, deeper into the unknown.

She knew she was falling down; the direction was clear. Yet it felt different from falling off a tree—or a horse. In many ways Emma felt as if everything was in slow motion—the fire reaching up to touch her, the snakes lunging at her, the churning waters, the motion of falling itself. She waited and waited—for a sharp thud, a sudden jerk as her body connected with something. Anything.

But it never came.

Instead, a fog slowly lifted from her body. Her ears were the first to gather information and send it her brain which, in turn, received the information and registered the sounds as familiar and nearby. The sounds then were given a label: chirping. A more distinct label was added immediately: birds chirping.

Emma opened her eyes. Even before she moved her head, she knew exactly where she was.

The forest.

Grams' forest.

In one motion, Emma's eyes found the path leading out of the forest at the same moment her legs received the instructions from her brain to move—no, to run. Even as she ran, she knew she wasn't running away from something. The shape-shifters were gone; the crown had defeated them. No, Emma was instead running toward something. Grams.

And then she saw her.

Lila Campbell laid in a crumpled heap at the edge of the forest floor, her head slightly turned to one side. Her hands were stretched out. Her skin was white, her sunken eyes closed. A trickle of blood traced the side of her temple. Emma knelt down and touched her face.

"Grams?" Emma said gently, but there was no response. The pale skin was deathly cold, and Lila's clothes were soaked through from the rainfall the night before.

"Grams, wake up," Emma urged, her heart beating faster. She shook Lila by the shoulders, but again, there was no movement. "Come on, Grams! Wake up!" The elderly woman lay limp on the ground.

This can't be, Emma's mind screamed. I've gone through so much—I've learned so much—in the last two days, all so that I could come back here and save Grams. There must be something else I can do.

Emma looked down at the woman unconscious on the grass. What could she do? Was it too late to save Grams?

That's when it hit her. The bag the fairies had made for her held the key. Emma quickly opened the bag. A pungent, sweet scent greeted her.

Lavenias.

At the time, Emma had thought Kia had been crazy to pick the deep purple flower and put it away for later use. Now, as she quickly pulled out a handful of purple blossoms, she was silently thanking the wise fairy.

Emma quickly crushed a handful of flowers in her hand, and then pressed the mixture against Lila's forehead, covering the gash on the side of her temple. At first, nothing happened. Then, like a glimpse of the sun's ray peeking through after a fierce thunderstorm, the flower's magic began to work.

The first clue that something was indeed happening was the change in Lila's color. The stark white skin slowly took on a pinkish hue that started in Lila's face and traveled ever so slowly down her neck, and then continued out to her arms and fingers, legs and toes. The deep sunken shadows around her eyes gradually disappeared, replaced with tiny lines that offered hints of natural aging. Even the gash itself appeared to have healed miraculously, disappearing altogether, the thin trail of dried blood the only sign that it had even existed. Emma noticed for the first time as well Lila's quiet breathing.

Grams was alive.

"Grams," Emma said as she bent down close. She stared down at the old woman. "Grams, can you hear me? Open your eyes." There was a stir, a flicker of movement, and suddenly Lila's eyes opened. They searched for a moment, trying to focus, and then rested on the sight of Emma.

"Emma…" Lila breathed. She tried to sit up, but Emma stopped her.

"Grams, you need to rest," Emma urged, gently guiding her back to a supine position. Lila did not argue, but quietly watched as Emma wiped away the dried blood. She reached out for Emma's other hand, clasping it in her own.

"Ouch!" Emma winced at the sudden pain in her hand. She pulled away and looked down at her palm. There, where the crown had been, was a deep red burn in the shape of a small circle. How strange that she hadn't noticed it before. Although the crown was gone forever, the symbol emblazoned on her hand haunted her. Lila's hand reached up to touch the cut on Emma's cheek.

"We are both hurt," Lila said as she sat up. "Help me into the house, dear girl." Emma helped her grandmother stand, and slowly, with her arm around the old woman's waist, they walked to the house.

Emma waited until Lila had finished her second cup of tea before she spoke. The pain from the burn on her hand had faded, thanks in part to the herbal mixture Lila had made using the plants already available in the kitchen. Lila was busy applying a small compress to Emma's cheek. Both granddaughter and grandmother were sitting at the kitchen table, wrapped in towels, slowly drying off from the cold rain.

Emma took a deep breath and broke the silence. She chose her first words carefully.

"Grams, I know about £areä." Emma watched as her grandmother processed the words. The old woman's eyes searched hers, as if looking for a glimpse of a past long lost and, upon finding it, allowing the river of emotions that had been suppressed for so many years to finally flow. Too many years had passed. Too many years.

Tears flowed down Lila's cheeks in a steady pattern as she silently wept, clutching her teacup in one hand, covering her trembling lips with the other. Emma didn't have to ask what the tears stood for; she knew what they meant. Del had been wrong.

Lila remembered £areä after all.

When Lila could finally speak again, she turned to Emma. "You've been…to £areä? But how…?" she asked, both sadness and joy reflected in her voice.

Emma took a breath and then began her story. "When I told you that I found the ring—I mean, crown—and the wing, I left something out. I didn't tell you that I took them." Emma searched Lila's face for any signs of discontent or disappointment, but there were none. She continued. "I had the crown in my pocket when we were in the garden, and then when I went to the house, the cat got out and ran into the forest…"

"…and you went after her," Lila added. "I wondered why you would have gone into the forest in the first place."

Emma nodded. "It was fine—at first. But then this mist came and…" She shivered and stopped. Speaking about what had happened in the forest brought the memories back to life.

"The shape-shifters feed on fear," Lila said.

"I figured that out—after a while," Emma smiled. "Anyways, the fairies saved me and brought me through the portal. That's when I met Del."

Lila let out a soft cry and a second round of tears freely fell. She quietly patted her forearm as she pondered over the name.

When she could finally speak, she turned to Emma. "Del—how is he?"

"He's good, Grams," Emma said. Lila nodded in acknowledgement, gently caressing the side of her teacup. Emma continued. "He showed me £areä—it is beautiful. I met the other fairies, and they had a special celebration. It was amazing! There were fireflies that lit up the sky, and flower petals that seemed to float in the air. Just remembering it isn't half as beautiful as it was being there." A tiny spark lit up Lila's eyes as Emma described £areä.

"Del also told me about the forest, and how you were hurt." Emma watched as the memories played across Lila's face. Excitement, surprise, fear, and sadness each took their turns showing a glimpse into the past. Lila sipped her tea, lost in thought.

"Why didn't you mention something, Grams?" Emma asked. "Why didn't you say something about your life?"

Lila laughed. "Dear child, you already think I am crazy. Why should I add to your thoughts with outrageous stories?" As she reached out to pat Emma's hand, she winked. Lila's words weren't said with malicious intent; they were true, and Emma knew this. Her perception of her grandmother had been one of a silly, old woman who lacked social skills. If Emma had been told a story half as crazy as the adventure she just lived through, she would have insisted on her grandmother receiving professional help. No, believing any ridiculous claims that Lila was once a fairy would not have been a possibility.

"I did not say anything for a number of reasons," Lila started. "To be believed was not important to me. What was important was to protect the ones I loved." Lila noticed Emma's confused look, so she continued. "When I was first hurt, I didn't understand how my life would change. I did not know that, because I only had one wing, I could not survive as a fairy anymore. Your grandfather gave me good care—the best care. I just thought I would get better. But fairy wings are not replaceable." Lila paused for a moment.

Emma knew how adventurous Lila had been in £areä. Her freedom had been so important to her. To take away her inner spirit would be to take away her soul.

"Oh, I could have returned to £areä," Lila said, "but what good would I have been? I was to be the chosen High Councilor, and I could not even lead the people. I could not fly. To a fairy, flying is like breathing." She gazed out the kitchen window, and then turned to Emma. "Dark days those were, my dear. Dark days…I did not understand why I was spared—why I did not just die on the forest floor. There were days I wanted to die, be assured. But one thing kept me going."

Gramps?" Emma asked. Lila nodded.

"He cared for me in a way I had never known," Lila said, a soft smile on her face. "He was patient and kind. He gave me a reason to live."

Love is patient. Love is kind.

How ironic that we both have learned a lesson on love, Emma thought. And in such different ways. Lila went on.

"I did not realize it at first," Lila continued. "Small signs there were—a laugh, the look in his eyes, my hand touching his, my heart beating. Finally, one day I made my decision. I chose Garret. I chose love."

"And you kept the crown and the wing?" Emma asked.

"I kept them, of course," Lila said. "They were a part of my life, a link to my past. I hid them away so that no one could find them. In the wrong hands, the crown would be dangerous. As long as I—or any other fairy—did not touch it, the shape-shifters would not know where I was, and £areä would be safe. Knowing that both the crown and the wing were in the house was a reassurance, I suppose—a way to remember my past. Although, I didn't expect you to find them, Emma."

Emma felt a twinge of guilt. How different things would have been had she not discovered the items in the dusty, old attic just two days ago. She would have stayed at her grandmother's house, living her usual life, waiting impatiently to go back to her own home. She would have been alone.

No, that isn't it, she thought to herself. She was thankful she found the items. After all, they led her to a new understanding of her dad and grandmother, something she treasured even more now. She didn't deny that the experience in £areä had left her scared and confused. But she had also gained important gifts—courage, trust, and gratitude. And most of all, love. Things were so different now. She was so different now.

"Did you ever talk about it with Gramps?" Emma asked. "You know, about your life before?"

"At first, perhaps," Lila said, "but then easier it was to simply embrace my new life. And then there was James, and the past was just that—the past."

Lila thought for a moment, and then turned to Emma. "Does Del…remember me?"

"Yes, he does," Emma said. "Grams, you were his sister. No, you still *are* his sister." The old woman let out a faint cry and covered her eyes, allowing a new batch of tears to flow.

"I was so worried," Lila explained. "I thought they would feel forsaken by my choice."

Emma simply listened to Lila's words. She knew that Del had suffered pain from Lila's choice to leave £areä forever. There were things he had not known—he still didn't know, and the act of not knowing caused pain itself. She also knew that had Lila returned to £areä, she would have died. Oh, maybe not physically, but her spirit would have slowly faded away, and Emma knew that, for her grandmother, that would be an end in itself.

"And…my father?" Lila asked. Emma shook her head. Lila was silent for a moment.

"I suspected as much," she finally said. "And Del is the High Councilor now?"

Emma nodded.

"That is very good for the fairies," Lila said. "He has the ability to lead, and lead well. Something I never had."

Lila took Emma's hand and looked at the palm. The scar from the crown held a faint pinkish clue that suggested healing.

"And what was your role in all of this?" Lila asked. Emma slowly exhaled and told her.

For the next hour grandmother and granddaughter talked of fairies and faraway kingdoms, having courage and learning to trust, and overcoming fear itself. Lila explained the uniqueness of fairy wings and special gifts, what it was like to enter a new world, and how she longed to see £areä just one more time. Emma peppered her grandmother with questions, and Lila answered them all with patience and thoroughness. Her aged eyes sparkled as she explained her fairy life to her granddaughter, being sure to include details that Emma had missed in her short visit to the fairy land. With each word the bond between the two strengthened.

"I must say, it is so nice it is to speak of £areä with someone again," Lila said as she sipped her tea. "For so long I did not talk about that magical place. I am thankful that you know about it now, too, my dear."

"Grams, I'm not the only one who knew about £areä," Emma said. Lila's brow furrowed in puzzlement. "My dad knew. He went there."

"What?" Lila cried. "How…?" The shock of the news caused Lila to stop mid-sentence.

Emma told her about finding the journal in the attic, and reading the entries. She explained how a young boy ventured into the forest to find his baseball and stumbled upon a place so magical, it lingered in his mind long after the experience itself faded away.

"I remember that day," Lila said finally, shaking her head. "I was so worried when I couldn't find him, so worried that the shape-shifters had found us and had figured out another way to enter £areä. But then up to the house he came. His baseball was in his hand. He never said anything."

"He wouldn't," Emma said. "He was just a boy, Grams. The memory of his experience faded over time. Later on, he thought that he was just writing about a silly dream he had had, not about something he had actually experienced." Emma thought for a moment, puzzled. "Grams, why were you able to remember everything about £areä, and yet Dad wasn't?"

Lila Campbell smiled a smile that reached deeply into her eyes. "My whole life was there. That is all I knew. You never truly forget who you are, my dear. Time might be the enemy, but love is stronger."

It made sense. £areä was who Lila was. James had only spent a sunny summer afternoon exploring the magical place.

"So, does this mean that I will forget?" Emma asked. "I don't want to."

"Not if we talk about it," Lila smiled. "I don't see any harm in that, now that the crown has been destroyed. But this must just be between us—our secret." Emma nodded in agreement.

The sound of a car door interrupted the conversation. A silent, knowing look between grandmother and granddaughter caused sudden movement in the kitchen just as Trudy Campbell entered.

"Greetings!" Lila slowly made her way over to hug her daughter-in-law. Although she was feeling better, her appearance did not go unnoticed.

"Oh, no!" Trudy said. "What happened?"

Emma looked at Lila, and then jumped in. "We got caught in the rain, and then Grams fell." Well, it was the truth…sort of.

"Don't you worry now," Lila reassured a worried Trudy. "I am feeling much better now, thanks to Emma's care. She has a way of taking care of me." Emma caught Lila's wink and smiled as Trudy took in the scene.

"I am certainly glad to hear that," Trudy said, studying her daughter for a moment. "How about you go get your things from upstairs? I have to get home to sort through all of the information I gathered this weekend." Emma nodded and obliged, thankful to be away from her mother's curious gaze.

As she entered her room, she stopped. The bed was still made, untouched. The comic books and journal were in the old box next to her bed. Her backpack with the wooden box hidden inside was sitting on the chaise lounge.

It isn't right for me to take the wing, Emma thought. It's a part of Grams, a part of her life before. She carefully put the wooden box containing the treasured item on the nightstand. She then picked up the journal and slowly thumbed through the now familiar pages, tucking it in her backpack when she was done.

As Emma and Trudy Campbell walked out to the SUV sitting in the driveway, Emma turned to catch one last glimpse of the scene. Lila Campbell was standing by the doorway, waving. Behind the house was the garden. The beautiful garden, with birdhouses and wind chimes. The vivid colors of the flowers played out against the darker greens of the forest.

And then she knew.

She knew why Grams had lived on the edge of the forest all these years. She knew why Grams hadn't moved—couldn't move—away. This was her home. This was her £areä. The flowers, and birdhouses, and wind chimes all offered a sense of comfort as she had tried to navigate the rules of a new world.

Sitting in the SUV as it made its way down the driveway, Emma smiled.

She knew that she was part of that new world, too.

EPILOGUE

Emma couldn't sleep. No matter what she tried—turning a different way, drinking water, thinking of something relaxing—sleep would not come.

She reached over to turn on the nightstand light. The faint glow filled the space directly beside her. She caught a glimpse of the comic books on the edge of the floor. On the top of the pile was the journal.

Emma reached for the leather book and opened it to the first page. By now, the passages had become familiar, a way of connecting with her father. The comforting words rose up from the page, enveloping her for the next hour.

The boy does what any boy would do—he goes into the forest to get his baseball. But then there is a swarm of butterflies surrounding him, and he follows them. They are all different colors, and I guess, if you were a girl, you would even say they were "pretty" although you didn't hear me using that word, ok?

Anyway, the butterflies lead the boy far into the forest. He comes to this open clearing and he stands there. Just then, there is glowing light, and then a bright flash and

Emma stopped. She wondered if James had been scared. Did he know what was happening? Did he understand what £areä really was, or was he simply accepting of the experience? She flipped through the pages, and started reading again—her favorite passage.

The boy is gone for a long time. Well, I should explain that it feels like a long time, but it is in fairy time. It doesn't match up with real world time. (Does that make sense? If it doesn't, oh well. I'm just telling a story here.)

So, the boy gets a little nervous. I think he is worried that his mom is going to find out and he will be in big trouble, so the fairies send him on his way. Not completely—they keep an eye on him because they are flying high up in the trees. He is walking through the forest, and that's when something strange happens.

He meets a girl.

She is older than he is—maybe twelve or thirteen. She is kind, and even though he really doesn't know her, he feels safe with her. They talk and play and walk, and just do stuff normal kids in a normal world would do, not thinking about the fact that they are in a totally different world.

When it is time to go, the boy is sad. He is afraid that he won't see her again. He is scared that he won't remember her. He wants to remember something about her because she was his first friend.

And that's when he knows.

He will remember her name.

Emma. Emma. Her dad had remembered one thing from £areä, and it was her name. A tear fell from the corner of her eye as she continued reading.

The boy hugs the girl, and he says "Thank you." She says it, too, and that's when it happens: a bright light, a loud cry, and he is back in the forest by his house. The girl isn't there anymore. He looks, but she is gone.

His mom is calling him, and he goes.

But he is happy.

He has a friend.

Emma closed the journal and held it to her chest. So many memories, some remembered, some lost forever. She turned her hand up and studied the tiny, faint scar on her palm. The memories of the crown and the shape-shifters had faded over the past weeks. Emma knew, though, that somehow, the faint reminder of how she entered £areä in the first place would always be there.

Suddenly, Emma sat up in bed.

The crown. Del had said that both the crown and her royalty had been the key to entering £areä. The crown was the reason the shape-shifters had chased her.

So, I had the crown, Emma thought. That is why I was able to enter £areä. But what did Dad have? She quickly scoured the journal pages, looking for clues. But they weren't there. It was plain and simple.

James never had the crown.

Then how did Dad get into £areä? Emma pondered, the open journal on her lap. Of course, he was royalty. But he didn't have the crown. Grams had hidden the crown and the wing to prevent him from ever finding them. What did he have?

And then Emma knew.

There was another way into £areä.

And she was going to find it.

AUTHOR'S NOTE

I once heard an author say that, in every story written, there can be found glimpses of the author. Sometimes the parts are hidden, woven within the intricacies of the story itself. Other times, the parts are blatant and in the forefront. The best stories have a mixture of both.

Yes, there are parts of me within this story. (No, I have never been a fairy, nor do I ever plan to be—just for clarification.) I will share with you, the reader, a few of my personal links and how I wove them into *Forbidden*.

    *   I love to work in my garden and play a part in making things grow. I must admit, however, that I am a bit jealous of Lila. My personal touch isn't nearly as successful as hers. My favorite flowers are delphinium, peonies,

coreopsis, lilies, and roses—all of which auditioned and made it into the book.

* Like Lila, I have a calico named Scout. Scout usually can be found sleeping beside my computer as I type away. She tends to somehow enter a story that I write, but then leaves just as quickly. Her deepest desire is to have a biography written about her life (a bit of foreshadowing here, readers!).

* Like Emma, I have lost my father, too. Although I was much older, the emotions surrounding the loss were the same. To be honest, some of the scenes where Emma struggled with the finality of her father's passing were the hardest to write, but also the most rewarding as they showed how Emma grew in the midst of hardship.

* Yes, even I struggle to have courage, trust, and gratitude. Do you?

Many thanks go out to:

My Grandmas—So thankful for grandmas that taught me how to bowl, knit, play Aggravation, make a mean scrambled egg and, most of all, how to enjoy each other's company.

First Reader Club (Iva, Lisa, Liz, Alisa, and Eliza) —Once again you have kept me on track, friends. You did a fabulous job asking hard questions, digging deeper, and truly challenging me to create a story that shows transformation. Thank you for reading and rereading and rereading until I got it right. I value your insight!

Michelle Reinhold—So thankful for your talent in areas I fall short in!

My family—Once again, you have supported me through this project. Thank you for your never-ending encouragement.

You, the reader—Believe it or not, you play an important part in this book. I write so that you can laugh and cry. I write so that you won't want to turn out the light at night, but keep going to see what really happens. I write so that you get that good feeling all over when you reach the end of the book, and you just can't help but smile. I would love to hear from you. Do you have questions for me? Ideas for future books? Want me to visit your class for an author talk or a skype session? Contact me at www. krburgbooks.com. I try to answer every email I get in a timely manner.

So thankful for the gift of writing and the ability to use it in this way—Col. 3:23

Forsaken
Book 2
coming Spring 2016

www.krburgbooks.com